D1425370

SCEPTRE

Also by Robert Girardi

Madeleine's Ghost
The Pirate's Daughter

Vaporetto 13

ROBERT GIRARDI

SCEPTRE

Copyright © 1997 Robert Girardi

First published in the United States of America in 1997 by Delacorte
Press, a division of Bantam Doubleday Dell Publishing Group, Inc.
First published in 1998 by Hodder and Stoughton
A division of Hodder Headline PLC
A Sceptre Book

The right of Robert Girardi to be identified as the Author of
the Work has been asserted by him in accordance with the
Copyright, Designs and Patents Act 1988.

10 9 8 7 6 5 4 3 2 1

A CIP catalogue record for this book is available
from the British Library

ISBN 0 340 70717 8

Printed and bound in Great Britain by
Mackays of Chatham PLC, Chatham, Kent

Hodder and Stoughton
A division of Hodder Headline PLC
338 Euston Road
London NW1 3BH

*Look at it, peering with its cold smile
into the blue decayed glass.*

—Osip Mandelstam

vaporetto (vắ-pə-reť-ō), *n.*
A motorized water taxi; steam engine. Commonly
used in Venice, Italy.

1

ELIZABETH LAY PANTING on the steel table, her yellow eyes dark with fear. Dried blood stuck with hair streaked the runnels, the air was thick with antiseptic fumes. She struggled to get up; I held her down with both hands as the assistant administered the muscle relaxer. A small cry caught in Elizabeth's throat when the hypodermic needle pierced her skin, a single forlorn note answered by the remorseful caw of a parrot through the thin walls of the examination room.

"They know, they always know," the assistant said darkly, and dropped the spent needle into a pedal-operated chrome garbage can. She was a wiry teenage girl with spiky blond hair and six earrings in each ear. She wore thick-lensed Buddy Holly glasses and a dog collar around her neck, perhaps to show her solidarity with the animals. Her lab coat was streaked with brown stains, a button stuck into one lapel announced that she was a FRIEND OF PETA, and that MEAT IS MURDER. Another button urged me to FREE THE CRUSTACEANS and showed a lobster escaping from a pot of boiling water.

"How long do we have to wait?" I said, trying to sound as calm as possible, but she could hear the agitation in my voice.

"Chill, Mr. Squire," she said. "Steve is cleaning up from the last one. Kind of a mess. A big German shepherd that got mashed crossing 95. Some people"—she hesitated and her eyes slid away from me—"don't take good care of their animal companions."

1

Elizabeth twisted under my grip and I began to sweat. The muscle relaxer didn't seem to be working. Suddenly, a series of shrill musical notes sounded from my jacket pocket—two long, two short, two long, two short.

"That your beeper?" the assistant said.

"It's not a beeper, exactly," I said.

"What is it then, a portable phone?"

"It's a market watch."

The notes sounded again. A drop of sweat formed between my eyes and dripped down the bridge of my nose. It took an act of will to keep from letting go of the cat to check the digital readout.

"You should have left that thing at home," the assistant said, frowning.

"Impossible, I'm an FX trader, my work depends on it."

The assistant looked puzzled. "You do special effects, like for the movies?"

"No." I attempted a smile. "Foreign exchange. I trade in international currencies for a bank. Reuters—that's the news service—sends an electronic message every time something happens that might affect the exchange rates, and the market watch receives a signal and sounds off. It could be a flood in China, the death of a world leader, higher interest rates for home loans . . ."

The assistant held up her hands. "Hey man, save it for later. You should really be dealing with your cat right now. Why not pick her up, give her a hug. You won't ever get the chance again."

"She doesn't like to be picked up," I said. "She likes to come to you." But after a minute, I picked up Elizabeth with some effort—she was a big female longhair, part Maine coon, part everything else, weighing almost sixteen pounds—and for once, she didn't protest or try to jump down. She went slack and laid her head along my arm and began to purr loud enough for the assistant to hear. I cradled her against the jacket of my eight-hundred-dollar Brooks Brothers suit, feeling absolutely rotten.

"See, that's sweet," the assistant said. "How long have you had the poor kitty?"

"She's almost eighteen now, she was my mother's cat," I said, talking fast, "you could say I inherited her when my mother died. But the cat never liked me, she never liked anyone but my mother. And now she's got diabetes, I have to give her shots of insulin every day, you know, it's very difficult, she scratches, she bites. And my fiancée is allergic to cats, her throat swells up whenever she comes into the house. And there's another thing, I'm going out of the country for six months for my bank. . . ." My voice trailed off. I set Elizabeth back on the table and she spread out in a relaxed puddle of fur and began to lick her white paws.

The assistant looked down at the cat and back at me, eyes narrow through the thick lenses of her glasses. "You mean there's nothing really wrong with this cat and you're having it put to sleep?"

"There's the diabetes," I said. "And she's old. How many years does she have left? Six months in a kennel would kill her."

The assistant crossed her arms. "You're really despicable," she said quietly. "I take my cat in twice a week for kidney dialysis and she just turned twenty. You're murdering your cat because she's an inconvenience. That's just despicable."

Before I could respond, the vet came in wearing a clean lab coat with the sleeves rolled up to the elbows. He was a hairy man. Hair grew out of his ears and his nostrils and connected his eyebrows in a continuous bridge.

The assistant turned and walked quickly past him through the swinging doors. "This one's all yours, Steve," she said. "Don't need me here."

The vet nodded at me blandly and went over to the stainless steel cabinet in the corner, its shelves cluttered with bandages, swabs, forceps, and other medical supplies. He took a long hypodermic needle from a black case and filled it with a solution from a small bottle marked with the skull and crossbones and stepped over to the table.

"Last week one woman brought in a violin and played it while her cat died," the vet said. "The animal apparently really enjoyed violin music, particularly Mozart. It died very peacefully. Any last words you'd like to say to your cat?"

"No," I said. "Let's get on with it."

I pushed Elizabeth down against the table again, and this time she did not struggle. She rolled over on her side like a ship run aground and held one paw in the air, purring. The doctor felt along the thick fur of her belly for an artery.

"I like to get them near the heart," he said. "Quicker that way." He took a roll of fat between his fingers and inserted the needle. I closed my eyes. Elizabeth made a sharp noise and a jolt ran through her and into my fingers. When I opened my eyes a minute later, she was still alive, her breath coming in a raspy panting. She turned her head toward me, and it seemed her yellow eyes held the answer to a secret that had been plaguing me since my mother died. Too late. I watched as the light faded there, and felt her body go limp in my grasp.

"She's gone now," the vet said gently. "You have several options for the corpse. If you want to keep the ashes, we can cremate her in a private ceremony for one hundred and seventy-five dollars, that price includes the urn. If you're not interested in keeping the ashes, we can cremate her communally for seventy-five dollars, or—"

"How much if I bury her in the backyard?" I interrupted.

"Fifty dollars," the vet said, frowning. "That's the price of the visit."

I took Elizabeth's body, wrapped in a blue plastic bag the vet assured me was odorproof, and put the bag in the trunk of my Saab Turbo. That evening, after I left the bank, I sealed the bag in a metal biscuit box weighed down with stones, wrapped the box with speaker wire, and punched holes in each side with a screwdriver. As the last streak of red faded from the sky in the west, I drove over to the waterfront in Southeast. There, a half mile above the Navy Yard, a narrow canal branches off the Anacostia and dead-ends between a tire warehouse and a closed Pepsi bottling plant. The water of the canal was still and black in the industrial light.

I stood on the edge of the embankment, took the biscuit box in both hands, and flung it out into the center of the canal. The loud splash echoed against the dull brick sides of the buildings. Immediately the box tipped to one side and began to fill with water, and in less than fifteen seconds it had sunk below the surface and was gone. Hands in the pockets of my trousers, I stood for a minute watching the subsiding ripples, a late moon rising over the tire warehouse.

"She was sick and old," I said to myself, "and she never liked me." But these words did not relieve the unaccountable pressure on my heart, the secret conviction that I had just committed a terrible crime. Just then, my market watch began to beep, two long, two short, like the tolling of guilt itself. I hurried back to the Saab and drove back to my town house in Arlington Mews. When I sat down at the kitchen table with a shot of Glenkinchie on the rocks to check the digital readout, my hands trembled: *FX trader murders cat, dollar plummets.* No. *Civil war in Liberia. Hundreds killed, heavy fighting, Monrovia.*

Bad news for any fool trading in Liberian dollars.

2

PANGLOSS WAS A SMALL, elegant establishment on P Street, done up in blond wood and oriental carpets, with no more than ten tables and a menu that changed every day. Handcrafted cuisine, according to *The Washingtonian*, was the latest dining trend inside the Beltway. The waitress sat down with us to explain the menu. She was an attractive girl who wore no makeup; her unconventional waitress outfit consisted of a colorful peasant dress, Birkenstocks, and homemade earrings.

"The fish is very good tonight," she said. "Chilean sea bass, it's a very firm fish and very fresh. And the veal is nice. But I wouldn't recommend the venison unless you really like game. This recipe, with a raspberry sauce, really allows the gamy taste to come through." She went down the menu, appetizers to dessert, discussing each dish in the same candid manner. We weren't patrons at a very expensive restaurant, it seemed, but guests at the house of a friend who loved to cook.

After we had made our selections and chosen the

wine, the waitress went off to discuss matters with the chef. Cynthia watched her go, then reached under the table and squeezed my thigh. Cynthia looked fine to-night. Her hair, glossy and black, was pulled smartly over one shoulder, her body in perfect physical shape. She jogged and played tennis and had been on the varsity women's crew at Michigan. Tonight she wore a simple square-collared dress of gray-blue silk. Everyone who knew her said she was a good catch.

"Don't you love it here?" she said. "The treatment you get is so personal. They want to be absolutely sure that you have a great meal."

Warren grunted from across the table. "You pay enough," he said. "They damn well better make sure you have a great meal."

His wife, Karen, hit the padded shoulder of his jacket with her small fist. She was already slightly drunk from her predinner cocktails at the bar. "Can't you ever think about anything but the bottom line?" she said. "You're a jerk! Look at this place. It's really charming. Perfect for Jack's good-bye dinner. Don't you think Jack?"

"Yes," I said. "Thanks for suggesting it."

"What the hell," Warren said. "Capitol Guaranty's picking up the tab."

The food, when it came, was excellent; on the wait-ress's advice, no one had ordered the venison. The women talked about politics a little self-consciously, then about patio furniture and dogs with more authority. Cynthia was a dog person. She wanted to get a collie after we were married and I sold the town house in Ar-lington Mews for something with three acres of yard and a rumpus room, out near Herndon. "Just think, Jack!" she said. "A big fluffy collie, like Lassie!"

I didn't know what to say to this.

7

Warren and I left them eating dessert and went over to the bar, a glossy half moon of blond wood in front of the window overlooking the traffic of P Street. He wanted to talk a little last-minute business over a *digestif*, he said. He was a big, meaty man with a thick neck and a large head of silvering hair. He had a sports background, had played college football at Tulane in the early seventies, and was in the habit of giving last-minute pep talks. He ordered an expensive eau-de-vie from the wan Korean barmaid. She put down two glasses and poured two healthy shots.

"Refills are on me," she said, smiling, but I could see her mind working: Best to keep the high rollers happy.

Warren raised his glass. "I suppose I should say *chin-chin*, isn't that what they say over there?"

"Yes," I said, *"chin-chin."* The stuff burned on the way down, and had a sour aftertaste. It was called Domaine de la Tour de Folie and came in a blue glass bottle shaped like a fish.

"Odd name for the stuff," I said, examining the label. "Tower of Madness Estates."

Warren smiled. "That's exactly why you're my point man," he said. "You're someone who notices every damn detail. You've got eyes that look beyond your trading screen. Some of these guys in the Room, and I won't mention any names, all they see is little arrows flashing up and down, dollar signs. One click, two clicks. You see the big picture. I know it's been tough on Cindy postponing the wedding, but the bank needs you on the ground there at least until the elections."

Warren was Capitol Guaranty's FX manager, with a better record in the win column than anyone at the bank, but he still had the college athlete's naive respect for anyone who had read a book. Actually, it had been years since I'd read any book cover to cover. My under-graduate education in the Great Books program at St. John's in Annapolis had left me with a passing knowl-edge of Aristotle, a smattering of Latin, and one of the few people in America who had actually finished William Harvey's lengthy treatise of 1628, the *Exercitatio anatom-ica*, in which that eminent physician first posited the cir-culation of the blood.

Of course, this sort of education makes a man unfit for the world. I had succeeded as an FX trader despite Plu-tarch and Montaigne and the rest, by exercising those very qualities the humanities deplored—namely, ruthless-ness, self-interest, and a single-minded devotion to mate-rial gain.

"How's your Italian these days?" Warren said, topping up my glass.

"Coming along," I said, though I had barely listened to the Berlitz tapes, one of which was now stuck in the faulty tape player in my Saab.

Warren leaned close. "What we're looking for Jack is a clear analysis of the scene, and I mean financial and po-litical. We're going to want monthly reports, full of good, juicy stuff. You know how volatile their economy is. Af-ter the elections in April, who knows what's going to happen. We're putting a man in Milan at Credito Italiano, and of course Bill Snead's been at Banco di Roma for a while now. I don't mind telling you, we're planning a big push on the lira either way, long or short, the week of the elections. We need stuff that's going to make our decision that much easier. I know you're going to do a great job," and there was just the right hint of menace in his voice when he said this.

I choked down the last of my eau-de-vie, turning my glass upside down on the napkin when he went to fill it again. "What about the trading?" I said. "How do you want me to handle that?"

Warren shook his head. "Don't sweat making trades," he said. "Keep your hand in, of course. But we're not expecting any real numbers. This is an intelligence-gathering mission. Trading is information, you know that."

Over at the table, the women had finished dessert and were signaling the waitress for the check. I made a move to join them, but Warren hung back a moment.

"Let me give you a last piece of free advice, Jack," he said. "Keep your eyes open, get plenty of sleep, and don't fuck up." As he followed me over to the table, I could hear coins jangling a faint musical note in his pocket.

3

THE PAVEMENT STEAMED along P Street. Moisture beaded the windshields of the cars parked at the curb. It was not raining, but the humidity stood at nearly one hundred percent. There is nothing worse than the jungle heat of Washington in July.

"I can't stand it," Cynthia said, fanning herself with her hand. "Get me some AC."

The parking attendant, a squat Salvadoran man with a face like a shovel, brought the Saab around with a screech of brake. I tipped him two dollars and we got into the car, cranked on the air-conditioning and drove down P, and made a right onto Rock Creek. In fifteen minutes, we were on the Beltway headed north. We had booked a room for the weekend at a bed-and-breakfast in a two-hundred-year-old farmhouse in Harper's Ferry, overlooking the confluence of two rivers and a creek—the Potomac, the Shenandoah, and the Antietam. It was one of Cynthia's favorite places; the rooms were crammed with antiques and there was nothing to do but eat and have sex.

"What's wrong with the tape deck?" she said now, pressing the eject button.

"Don't fool with it," I said. "Try the radio."

She fiddled with the radio for a while, couldn't find anything she liked and turned it off.

"I shouldn't tell you this, because it could get Karen in trouble," she said. "But Warren's got his eye on you. He really likes you. She says they're thinking of moving you up to chief trader when you get back." She smiled and squeezed my arm; her teeth were perfect, a miracle of orthodontics. "It's not so bad postponing the wedding for that, is it Jack?"

I didn't say anything. Cynthia and Karen had been sorority sisters at Michigan. Cynthia and I met two and a half years ago in the bank's courtesy tent at the Virginia Gold Cup. There, the hotshot traders, board members, family, and assorted hangers-on gathered under the white-and-green-striped canvas to munch on shrimp wrapped in bacon, satay chicken skewers, and bite-sized quiches, drink decent domestic champagne and watch the horses go down over the jumps. The afternoon was beautiful, an ocean of undulating grass and yellow sunlight. I wore a crisp seersucker suit and bow tie, Cynthia a sundress with a pink and blue starfish print that showed off her cleavage, a floppy straw hat, expensive shades. We talked and drank champagne, and got a little drunk, and that night, she came back to my town house in Arlington Mews and we had sex on the living room carpet, then on the big bed in my room upstairs, Elizabeth watching with disapproval from her perch in the bookcase.

"Jack, you're not talking," Cynthia said now. The dark fields of West Virginia passed featureless out the window, haystacks lined up in rows like silent judges just beyond the throw of the headlights. "Is something on your mind?"

"No," I said. "Just tired."

"Come on, I can always tell when there's something on your mind."

"There's Elizabeth," I said. "I keep seeing her eyes."

Cynthia was silent for a moment. "You know that was inevitable," she said. "Stop torturing yourself. She was old and sick. I would have taken her in for you, but my allergies . . ."

"Yes," I said. "Let's not talk about it."

We reached the bed-and-breakfast in Harper's Ferry just before midnight. They gave us a stuffy corner room with a view of the Dumpsters in the backyard.

"I thought we were getting a room on the river side," Cynthia said. "I can't breathe in here." But in two minutes flat, she was out of her clothes and asleep on the high, uncomfortable bed.

I lay down in my Jockeys and a T-shirt on top of the sheets and woke gasping sometime after midnight from a dream of the old parade ground at St. Albert's Academy, in Lincoln.

In the dream, it was Founder's Day, all the cadets in parade dress, the parents assembled in the grandstands, my father fresh from the Pentagon in his dress blues standing stiff for the national anthem beside the Rector in the flag-draped VIP box. My uniform was impeccable, my brass buttons shining like gold, boots spit-polished to a mirror finish. Then, at the last minute, I looked down and realized in horror that I had managed to forget my pants. It was too late to run back to barracks and get them. The trumpet sounded, the whole corps advanced as one, and there I was marching up and down in the midst of the other cadets, bare-assed, penis swaying in time to the music, my father's eyes upon me, as a massive storm cloud in the shape of a cat's head blew across the prairie and over the parade ground with the inevitability of doom itself.

Cynthia and I did not have a very good time at the bed-and-breakfast that weekend. The weather was un-bearably hot, the sky low and oppressive, the mosquitoes biting. We fought over little things and made love only twice. The second time I was barely half hard inside of her.

"I've never been to Venice," she said over brunch on Sunday. "It sounds like a really interesting place. I'll come visit. You want me to come visit?"

I took a second too long finding an answer.

4

THE BANK RENTED ME an apartment that oc-cupied the entire top floor of the Palazzo Bragadino, a five-star hotel on the Grand Canal. The walls were deco-rated with four-hundred-year-old paintings and lozenges of inlaid marble, polished to a dull sheen. Heavy, gilt-edged velvet drapes hung over the row of arched win-dows that gave out on the picaresque traffic of gondolas, water-buses, and sleek, mahogany-hulled motor launches in the green water below. Room service could be summoned with the pull of a bell-rope. Still, the place was grandiose and uncomfortable, better suited as the residence of a duke and his retinue—which, in fact, it once had been—than as an apartment for a single American businessman.

I could not sleep in Venice. At first it was jet lag and an unfamiliar bed, then something more sinister. The beauty of the city was unsettling to my nerves. Every evening the sun dropped round as an onion behind the big green dome of the Salute, turning the Giudecca channel a fantastic shade of deep rose; the facades of the ancient, delicately crumbling palazzos glowed with muted sadness in this forlorn, beautiful light. It was unbearable. Beauty has a place, of course—between the pages of a book, in pictures on the walls of museums, in high and inaccessible mountain valleys—but a daily diet of beautiful things can be difficult for the aesthetic digestion. America's banal landscape of fast-food chains, malls, parking lots, high-voltage transformers, and glass-fronted office towers is, in the end, easier on the soul.

I tried working late to avoid the painful sunsets, but working late in Italy is impossible. The Venetians call the hour between six and seven p.m. *l'ora d'oro*, the golden hour, when the dying light paints the whole city the color of longing. The cafes in the Piazza San Marco are full of tourists, locals line the tin counters of the wine shops near the Rialto bridge, and students spill out along the fondamenta from the bars of the Misericordia. My office in the Comparini Bank, just a few steps south of the Piazza San Marco, emptied out at five-thirty exactly. To stay any later was to risk being locked in till the next morning.

This happened to me once, on Wednesday the last week of August. I worked through the night, trading pounds sterling on the Nikkei exchange in Tokyo, then lire and Belgian francs when the market opened in New York. As dawn began to show above the flagstones of the little courtyard outside my window, I spread some newspapers on the floor, balled my jacket into a pillow, and tried to sleep. I closed my eyes and dreamed of rowing, of dark gondolas rocking on the water of an unknown lagoon, until Vida, my Italian secretary, woke me at eight-thirty a.m.

"Signor Squire! You have been to work all night?" She pronounced my name *Squee-arhe*. I didn't have the heart to correct her. She was short and middle-aged, wore plain clothes and comfortable shoes, and reminded me of someone's maiden aunt. I rose from my newspaper bed, went to the bathroom, splashed water in my face, and returned to my desk for the opening of the exchange in Milan. I didn't feel all that bad. It was more sleep than I'd gotten in days.

Working conditions at the Comparini Bank were a little different from what I was used to. Back home at Capitol Guaranty, like everyone else, I had my place in the Room—a basketball court–size space full of screaming traders, each one equipped with four screens and a fifty-six-line board. Here, I had one screen and ten lines and shared a small office with only one other person, an excitable commodities broker named Rinio Donato. He was in his late twenties, a genuine native of Venice, as had been his father and his father's father and so on—of this birthright, he was quick to assure me—and a popular figure at the bank for reasons that had nothing to do with his abilities as a broker. All the women commented on his resemblance to the Italian actor Vittorio Gassman, which Rinio played for all it was worth.

Indeed, Rinio seemed more interested in women than in commodities trading. He spent half the day on the phone with any number of mistresses, though he had a wife at home, six months pregnant. It was easy to tell who he was talking to from the sound of his voice: The trading was obvious—he screamed, sweated, mopped his brow; the wheedling, cajoling tone, he reserved for his wife; the low, seductive murmurs were for the other women. One afternoon, he got into loud arguments with two of them in back-to-back phone calls. From what I could understand of these exchanges, he had broken a date with both to go out with a third—then the third called and canceled. When he hung up the phone at last, he was in tears.

"Everything going O.K. over there?" I said.

"It is so difficult," he sniffed. "I have a friend, her name is Carlota. . . ." Then he stopped himself, unsure of how much to tell me. Would I report his behavior to his superiors, perhaps even his wife? "But, excuse me, I do not mean to weigh you down with personal problems."

I smiled. "You know what the poet Pushkin said?"

He looked interested. "No, I do not," he said.

"It is not possible to sleep with all the women in the world, but you must try."

Rinio slapped his leg and laughed uproariously. His moods were as changeable as the moods of a child. "That is very good," he said. "Very good!" Suddenly, we were more than friends, we were coconspirators, secret agents on a mission of seduction in the City of Women.

5

BETWEEN THE HOURS OF three-thirty and six in the morning, the work barges dieseled up and down the Grand Canal, carrying cabbages and eggs, plastic sandals, condoms, rechargeable batteries, cases of beer, milk, fresh bread, toilet paper, pencils, cheese, new editions of the *Gazzettino* and the *International Herald Tribune*—all the mundane stuff needed for another day of city life. This is the reason why Venice is so expensive. Ordinary things like throat lozenges and duct tape must be brought over from the mainland, loaded on to the barges, then unloaded again. The inflation comes in portage fees.

The garbage scows chugged along behind the work barges, just before dawn. One of these scows idled in the canal for twenty minutes every morning below my window, the stench of diesel fumes and rotting garbage mixing with the damp air in the apartment. I tried closing the shutters, putting a pillow over my head, earplugs. I even tried dragging a blanket into the big marble tub in the bathroom and padding the door with towels. Nothing worked. Between the stench and the noise, I remained wide-awake, and in another half hour the canal was flooded with lucid morning light, all thought of sleep impossible.

Soon, I began to wake up automatically at three a.m. in anticipation of this watery cacophony—though no matter how early I went to bed, I could never fall asleep before midnight. I felt like one of Pavlov's dogs, trapped in a ridiculous state of self-conditioned wakefulness. Exasperated, I took to roaming the streets in the small hours of the morning. Anything was better than lying stiff and

17

rigid in the clammy sheets, waiting for the scow's inevitable arrival as the clock ticked one slow second after the next.

Perhaps the best way to get the true feel of any city is to walk its back alleys when everyone else is asleep. I soon discovered Venice is like an apple that looks great on the outside, but inside of which lives a giant worm. Away from the theater-backdrop facades of the Grand Canal, the expensive cafes of the tourist campos, the streets were narrow and poorly lit, the smell of mildew and rot persistent, the palazzos held together with heavy cables and makeshift scaffolding, sinking into the muck of the lagoon, their very stones permeated with the mold and damp of centuries.

During the course of my sleepless noctambulations over the first two weeks, I did not meet a single other human being. Only the cats emerged from nowhere in the darkness to do their business in the empty campos. There are thousands of stray cats in Venice, mostly odd-looking flat-faced tabbies, a few orange and white. Where they live during the day is a mystery, but after midnight, the city belongs to them. There is no sand or dirt anywhere, barely a single tree, every inch is paved over with ancient flagstones, and so the cats squat to shit and piss unnaturally against the walls of the buildings. At dawn, men in orange municipal jumpsuits come with big brooms to sweep the steaming mounds of cat shit into the canals.

With the right directions, it is theoretically possible to cross the city from the Bacini di Cannaregio to the Canale Scomenzera in forty-five minutes. In practice, however, the right directions are a matter of conjecture. Venice is made up of one hundred and eighteen separate islands, connected by narrow bridges that cross and re-

cross a thousand stagnant canals. A labyrinth of crooked
alleys and dead ends, many unmarked and nameless, must
be negotiated to reach a palazzo fifty yards away as the
pigeon flies. For my three a.m. rambles, I quickly learned
to set a specific destination—say the church of San Zanipolo, or the Basilica San Marco—then plot the course in
red pencil on a detailed map of the city. I always made
sure to bring along the map, neatly folded to the parame-
ters of my journey, and a handy pocket flashlight.

But one morning, half sick from lack of sleep, inevitably, I forgot both map and flashlight. Five minutes away
from the Palazzo Bragadino, I was already lost. I tried to
point my nose in the direction of the Grand Canal and
ended up more lost. I wandered around in the early
gloom completely disoriented, unsure even of which part
of the city answered the hollow echo of my footsteps.
There was no one to ask, no street signs. Everywhere I
looked I saw the crumbling facades, sagging into each
other at crazy angles. Above, the same featureless, hazy
sky.

After an hour of aimless wandering, I began to feel
claustrophobic and sat down in a doorway and put my
head on my knees. My eyes ached, I was slightly dizzy.
Even eyes closed, red squiggles floated at the edge of the
blackness. I hadn't slept more than three and a half hours
a night for weeks. How long before I collapsed from exhaustion, had to be medevaced back to the States? A
breakdown like that, in the middle of an important as-
signment for the bank, would be just the thing to end my
career with a bang.

As these grim thoughts descended upon me, I heard a
small mewing sound from close by. I lifted my head off
my knees and saw a kitten standing in the center of the
alley about ten feet away. It was black, which is rare for

Venice, no older than six weeks, with yellow eyes like Elizabeth's. The kitten stared up at me with its yellow eyes and mewed again, then ambled off around the nearest corner. For reasons I can't say, I rose and followed.

From up ahead came a vague feline rumble. The alley turned sharply at a ninety-degree angle and emptied out into a small campo whose damp pavement was covered with cats. They sprawled everywhere, numerous as pigeons, purring, fighting, licking their paws, chasing each other in and out of the shadows, hunched together in furry groups. A single streetlamp with a tin pie-plate shade hanging from a wire overhead blew back and forth in a wind that smelled of tar and rotting fish. The buildings on both sides were boarded up, a few blackened by the soot of a fire long past. At the center stood an ancient wellhead, capped with a rusting iron grate, and beyond that, a neglected Renaissance chapel, its heavy doors bolted against the night.

The kitten disappeared into the general mass of cat fur. Then the fishy wind shifted the lamp on its wire and I made out a woman crouching amidst the cats just the other side of the wellhead. Her back was toward me; she wore a voluminous black cloak, of the type called a domino, usually worn in Venice during the Carnival. The hood hung around her shoulders and her tightly curled blond hair shone in the wavering light. She was unwrapping newspaper bundles of fish guts and other food slop, and spreading them on the pavement for the cats. Several bundles lay open already; a few cats stood around this mess, quietly feeding. Most didn't seem to be in any hurry. Some sniffed at the food disdainfully, others lazily watched from the shadows.

I pushed through the cats, careful not to step on any tails. They jumped out of the way with a little whine of complaint, or hissed at the laces of my running shoes; one or two tried to rub their heads against my leg, nearly tripping me up in the process. As I got closer I heard the woman whispering. She was talking to the cats. I couldn't make out words, just a low sympathetic hush. I stopped short on the far side of the wellhead; I didn't want to startle her.

"*Scusi, parl'inglese?*" I called out to her. It was the only complete phrase I knew in Italian.

The woman set down her bundle of fish guts, paused for the length of a heartbeat. When she turned in my direction, I drew a sharp breath. Even in the dim light of the campo, her skin glowed with the sort of unnatural whiteness that used to be the result of bathing in arsenic. She was maybe twenty-eight or thirty; her dark eyes contrasted oddly with her dyed blond hair. They were black and seemed to reflect nothing at all.

"*Sì, inglese,*" she said at last. "I speak." Her voice held the low timbre of certain complicated wood instruments.

"I'm lost," I said. "If you could just point the way to the Piazza San Marco."

"Piazza San Marco, from here is difficult," she said.

"Maybe if you could tell me where I am. Then I can get my bearings."

"You are in the Campo dei Gatti," she said. "This means the Place of the Cats."

"Yes," I said, looking around. "I don't need to understand any Italian to figure that out."

The young woman's expression registered something halfway between amusement and complete disinterest. "You like the cats, signore?"

"I had a cat for years," I said, without thinking. "I had to have her put to sleep. Actually, she was my mother's cat. She was old, sick. . . ." I stopped myself, feeling foolish.

"Put to sleep?" the woman said, not understanding.

"That is, the veterinarian gives the cat an injection," I said, embarrassed, "and then it . . . it dies. . . ." My voice trailed off. It was an odd conversation to be having at four in the morning with a stranger in a campo full of cats.

"So you do not like the cats?" she said, frowning.

No one had ever asked me this question. My friends had always assumed that a man with a cat must like cats. "It's not that," I said at last. "With my job, I don't have much time for animals. Animals get lonely, just like people. I guess I wasn't home much at the end. I'm not saying I feel great about that."

The woman came around the fountain, cats rubbing themselves against her ankles, and studied me frankly for a long moment. "You are an American?" she said, then answered her own question. "*Sì, sì,* only an American would dress like this." She indicated my outfit with a wave of her white hand.

I had to agree: I wore a Nike "Just Do It" T-shirt, a zippered Chicago Bulls sweat jacket, turquoise and black running shorts, and a pair of Air Jordans. The typical gaudy mishmash of brand-name athletic wear favored by Americans at leisure.

"Also only an American would come to Venice with but a few words of Italian. Am I right?"

"You're right, about that one, too, unfortunately," I said, grinning.

"You seem an honest type," she said, then she nodded to herself. "Yes, I think so. Are you an honest type?"

I shrugged. I had many faults, but I liked to think that lying wasn't one of them. "I'm as honest as the next guy,"

I said. "But real, absolute honesty is nearly impossible—it all depends on the circumstances. Thank God I'm not in advertising."

"Yes, sadly, we live in a time of many lies," she said. "People, they prefer lies to the truth. It is good to tell the truth, I think. But even with that, one must be careful. There is a famous expression '*Le falsità non dico mai mai, ma la verità non a ogniuno.*' This is what Sarpi says. It means lies to no one, but the truth not to everyone. Do you know Sarpi?"

I said I didn't.

"He was a very great man, very wise and holy. Every Venetian they love Sarpi, because Sarpi, he loved Venice. He—"

In the next second, one of the cats let out a weird, unearthly wail that made me jump. The woman laughed, showing small pointed teeth.

"Do not be frightened," she said, then she stopped laughing and looked into my eyes for a long, disconcerting moment. "People say that cats are cruel, but they are not cruel. They are as God made them. Their souls are innocent. They will not harm you."

6

I FOLLOWED HER THROUGH a series of alleys and over black canals I would never remember. The woman walked quickly, not looking right or left, and seemed to know the way more by instinct than by sight. We came out somehow at the Riva del Ferro, and crossed up the steep steps to the summit of the Rialto bridge.

"Thanks a lot," I said. "I know where I am now."

"Yes," she said. "I will leave you here. But may I ask you a favor? Do you have an American cigarette?"

I don't smoke much, only when I'm nervous or waiting, but I found a pack of two-month-old Lucky Strikes in the pocket of my sweat jacket. The matches tucked into the cellophane were from the Old Ebbitt Grill in Washington. That place with its hearty steaks, microbrews on tap, and lobbyists eating lunch seemed as far away right now as Mars.

We stepped over to the parapet and I lit her cigarette and my own, the match flaring yellow in the predawn gloom. She threw one panel of the domino over her shoulder with a practiced gesture. Under it she wore a tight-fitting sleeveless turtleneck of gray wool and black jeans, and she wasn't wearing any shoes. I thought this strange, but I didn't say anything. One must suppose that they do things differently in Italy. Her bare feet looked very white against the dark stone.

"I'm afraid these are pretty stale," I said, blowing smoke over my shoulder.

She shrugged. "Anything is better than the Italian cigarettes." But when she drew the smoke into her lungs, she made a face. The old Luckies tasted like cardboard. For a few minutes we smoked in silence and looked down at the romantic sweep of the Grand Canal. The moon hung low, a fading sickle, upside down in the sky. The faint reek of a garbage scow floated on the wind.

"You see, I feed the cats every night," she said. "Oh, Venice everyone says, the home of many lovely cats. But if I don't feed the poor things, they will starve. Of course, there are so many cats in Venice, it is hard to feed them all. I go to the back doors of the restaurants when they close and collect the scraps. Everyone knows me, all the pot scrubbers and cooks. They think I'm crazy. They call me Signora dei Gatti. The Lady of the Cats or the Cat Lady, which is more correct?"

"Cat Lady, I guess," I said. "But Lady of the Cats has a certain ring to it."

"The poor cats must be fed, yes?"

It was a question that didn't need an answer. I flicked the bitter end of my Lucky into the Grand Canal and studied her sharp, elegant profile. Her face showed no wrinkles or lines. But there was a weariness about her gestures that suggested too much intense experience.

"So all night you feed the cats of Venice," I said. "What do you do during the day?"

"During the day I try to sleep," she said. "You see, sleep is very difficult for me, oh for many reasons. And during the day I am very, very tired. But always at night I am awake. This is the way I am. You are the same way, I think. You do not sleep, yes? Perhaps this is why you wander Venice in the dark? Is this right?"

"Fellow insomniac." I grinned. "There ought to be a secret handshake. But for me, it's just here, just in Venice. I sleep fine at home, or at least I used to."

"No, I think perhaps you are in love." She shot me a quick feline glance out of the corner of her eyes. "Perhaps you just have come from the apartment of a woman. Are you in love?"

"No, I'm not in love," I said.

She was about to speak, but she was distracted by a dim, scuttling movement—rats probably—along the bridge abutment below. Then she glanced up at the sky to the east where a tinge of pink showed in the blue-blackness. Dawn wasn't far away.

"Ah," she said. "I must go."

She stubbed her cigarette out on the old stone and

turned down the steps of the Rialto in the direction of the Fondamenta del Vin. Halfway down, she stopped. Just then a barge full of turnips rounded the corner from the direction of San Stae and passed noisily under the bridge, rattling the windows of the darkened palazzos. She waited for the sound of the diesel engine to die away before she turned back.

7

ON SUNDAY, RINIO TOOK ME on a tour of the lagoon in his Arkansas Traveller, an old sixties-era American-made inboard of the type I remembered from midwestern lakes of my youth. He had named her the *Serenissima*, but the vessel remained distinctly American, with a hull of red and white fiberglass, kitschy red leatherette seat cushions, chrome bar table, and oversize steering wheel of varnished Carolina ash.

"Friends of my father's had a boat like this!" I shouted over the burp and stutter of the exhaust. "Where did you get it?"

Rinio stood at the wheel, in a captain's hat and double-breasted yachtsman's blazer. "This is Venice"—he shrugged—"there are many boats."

His pregnant wife sat scowling beneath the striped foul-weather canopy aft, her knuckles white against the rust-flecked chrome railing. She didn't speak a word of English. Occasionally, Rinio would translate a piece of our conversation. She would nod at this, unsmiling, her eyes unreadable through huge black sunglasses.

"Your wife doesn't seem to be enjoying herself," I said.

"Maybe she doesn't feel well. Must be hard with the baby."

"My wife says I do not include her with my friends," Rinio said. "Now, I try to include her with my friends and she does not have a good time. You know what I think? I think she does not like the boats. Her father and grandfather, they did not like the boats. They were not Venetians, but from Mestre, Terra Firma." He waved in the direction of the mainland.

We negotiated the traffic of the Grand Canal and motored out through the Misericordia into the lagoon. The vast, shallow expanse of green water was sprinkled with islands, more than a thousand in all, Rinio said, some inhabited like Murano and Burano, most abandoned, their buildings sinking into ruins.

"The government tried to sell thirteen islands last year," he said. "But no one would buy. Who would want to live out here with the birds and the fishes?"

We stopped on Burano at a small trattoria run by one of Rinio's cousins. It was a pleasant place, with big yellow umbrellas on the patio outside overlooking the main street. Old women dressed in black sat in wicker chairs before the doorways of brightly painted houses across the way, heads bent over their lace making, long black needles clacking away.

"It is all for show," Rinio said. "These ladies do not sell enough lace to feed a cat for a week. The government pays them to sit there dressed like old women in an opera."

As we settled at a table on the patio, Rinio and his wife got into an argument. I couldn't follow any of the words that flew between them, but it was brief and intense, like a summer squall, and at the end of it, Rinio's wife got up in a huff and stalked down the street toward the boat.

"She's pregnant, she probably needs to eat," I said when she was gone. "Maybe you should go after her."

Rinio made an inarticulate gesture that meant no, never.

"What was the argument about?"

"My wife," Rinio said, shaking his head. "She is very difficult woman. She does not like my cousin. She says she will not eat here."

Rinio's cousin came out a few minutes later, carrying a plate of *bruschetta* and a bottle of Chianti. Later, he brought an eggplant dish, a salad of endive and marinated squid, and a bowl of fried pasta with chickpeas. He sat down with us at the table, and sipped a thimble-sized glass of grappa while we finished eating. He was a big man with meaty Popeye forearms and a thick head of curly hair. He looked nothing at all like Rinio. The two of them talked for few minutes, laughing and slapping each other on the back, then the cousin got up and returned to his kitchen.

"We always talk about women," Rinio said with a wink that was supposed to explain everything. "Once, my cousin, he arranged a date for me with his sister who is a beautiful girl. But my wife, she finds out"—he puffed his cheeks out—"it is a complicated story."

When the plates were cleared away and the espresso came, Rinio drew a small yellow map out of his pocket and unfolded it across the tablecloth. It was a map of Venice and the lagoon, showing the water bus lines in red, blue, and brown and various combinations thereof.

"This is for the vaporetto," Rinio said, tapping the paper. "Very important to you. You wish to know Venice, you must travel like the Venetians, on the vaporetto." He

spent the next twenty minutes explaining the intricacies
of the various lines. I faded in and out, only half interested—buses are tedious and slow means of transporta-
tion, even if they do run on water—I tried to suggest that
his wife was getting tired waiting in the boat, but he was
very insistent:

The main city lines 1 blue, 2 through 4 red, and 5
brown ran up the Grand Canal and around the island of
the Rialto; 18 and 12 blue, 7 black, and 5 ran out into
the lagoon from the Fondamenta Nuove. And there were
more than a dozen or so other permutations. Some went
out but didn't come back, some ran on weekends, some
didn't; others only ran on Sundays or holidays. In addi-
tion to the vaporettos, there were the ferries to Mestre
and Chioggia and the mainland.

"And here is the Lido." Rinio indicated the long green
strip of land between the city and the Adriatic. "To get
to the Lido, you take any of the lines 10 through 20 from
the Riva degli Schiavoni, or the 2 and 4, but only after
the Sant'Elena stop. You want to swim, you go to the
Lido. Here are the best beaches, here is also the Galop-
patoio. . . ."

"The what?"

"It is for the horses, to bet."

"Not for me," I said. "I do all my betting on the exchange market."

"Well." Rinio smiled. "You never know." He handed
me the map. "Now, do you have any questions?"

I examined the map closely, feigning interest. "What's
this place?" I said at last, pointing to a dark square of an
island directly opposite the Fondamenta Nuove in the
lagoon.

Rinio looked down and shook his head. "No, no. You
do not want to go there unless you are dead. It is the

Cimitero San Michele. If you die in Venice, they bury you on San Michele. But only for so long, unless your family pays more money. Then they dig you up and throw your bones into the lagoon."

At that moment, a shadow fell across the table. We looked up to see Rinio's wife standing there, arms crossed, her lips pressed into a hard line. She didn't have to say anything. Rinio folded the map quickly and put it away. Then we stood and without another word followed her down to the boat rocking impatiently in the water at the slip.

8

LATER THAT AFTERNOON, as the golden hour lit Venice the noisome color of every tourist's dreams, I walked up through the city to the Fondamenta Nuove. Sunday couples strolled arm in arm along this wide stone quay, mixing with the crowds of tourists disembarking at the vaporetto platforms. The far islands of the lagoon were lost in haze, but the funerary walls of San Michele just across the channel shone in golden light. They were built of dusky brick, topped with marble battlements and punctuated by disused watergates whose greening steps led down into the lapping water. The white turrets and crosses of the largest tombs were visible just over the wall, the black points of cypresses swayed idly in the wind.

I stepped into an English pub halfway down the fonda-menta and stood at the counter for a pint of bitters and watched the light fade from gold to red over the cemetery island, visited with a sensation I could not name.

For the first time in a long while, I thought of my mother, who died in a car accident when I was twelve. She was driving a brand-new used 1964 Corvair Monza convertible at the time, the dangerous model that Ralph Nader had declared unsafe at any speed. Somewhere in my collection of photo cubes, I still had a snapshot of this faulty machine, fresh from the used-car lot at Pallone Chevrolet, top down, hubcaps gleaming, steely flank a bright lemon yellow in the sun.

Not long after the snapshot was taken, Mom picked up a friend and drove the Corvair around the Beltway to Tyson's Corner for a little shopping. Coming home, down the curve of the exit ramp at the intersection of 95 and the Beltway at Springfield, the Corvair dropped its driveshaft, flipped over, and skidded belly-up into the guardrail. They had to scrape what was left of Mom off the scarred, oily asphalt; through some quirk of physics, the friend was thrown from the passenger seat onto the weedy shoulder and suffered only two broken ribs and a few miscellaneous bruises.

I was in my freshman year at St. Albert's then, a Catholic military high school in Lincoln, Nebraska, run by the Albertine Brothers, an order of warrior monks founded during the Crusades. Father wouldn't let me come east for the funeral because of midterms at school. By the time I got home at Easter break, the tombstone— a pitiful brass plaque no bigger than a notebook—was already tarnishing in a scrabbly field off Route 236 that passed for a cemetery, and crabgrass was growing over the grave. Other than myself, there was nothing left to mark Mom's passage in the world but a stack of tattered letters tied in fading ribbons, ten thousand dollars in T-bonds, a pile of clothes for the Salvation Army, and one cat.

Mom had gotten a kitten from the neighbors two months before the accident. She had sent me photographs of an adorable ball of fur with big yellow eyes: *If I can't give you a little sister right now*, she said in the accompanying note, *at least I can give you this little friend. She's waiting for you to finish school so you can give her a great big kitty hug. Her name is Elizabeth.* But after the accident, Father decided to give Elizabeth to the pound. I called in tears from the crackly dorm phone and begged him to keep her for me. I would take care of the kitten, I said, clean the litter box, everything—and in a rare moment of consideration, he agreed.

Eventually, I did everything I said I would, and more: I cleaned Elizabeth's litter box regularly, took her to the vet's for shots and deworming, bought Kibbles 'n Bits and cat toys out of my hard-earned allowance. But from the beginning, she was a cerebral, melancholy animal. She would not sleep with me, she slept in the basement on a scrap of Mom's old bathrobe; she turned her nose up at my cat toys, and she would not play with string or balls of tinfoil like other kittens. She seemed to prefer my father to me, a man who disliked cats as much as he disliked weakness and sentiment. No, Elizabeth never liked me, she never did.

9

THE *MARANGONA* RANG OUT twelve heavy strokes at midnight from the shadowy heights of the

Campanile. The wind buffeted the lights suspended on their skein of wires above the piazza. The strange facade of the Basilica San Marco was reflected like a mirage of a fairy-tale castle in black puddles along the pavement. Venice was sinking, everyone knew that, it was only a question of time.

I walked along, hands in my pockets, scuffing through the puddles like a kid. The lira had surged against the yen late in the day, and I had come out of it three million long for the bank. It was a good feeling, to know that you were doing what they paid you to do. I followed the arcade twice around; there was no sign of her. But just as I was about to give up and head back to the hotel, I felt a whisper on the back of my neck like the breath of a cat, and I turned around and there she was.

Tonight, she wore her black domino slung over both shoulders like a cape, and a curve-fitting cocktail dress of shiny red silk, cut low in the front. Black gloves reached to her elbows. I blinked my eyes. She wasn't exactly beautiful—still, there was something about her that made me want to look and keep looking.

"You didn't think I would come," she said.

"No I didn't," I said. "Especially when I realized yesterday I didn't know your name."

"I am Caterina Vendramin," she said and held out her gloved hand, palm down. I wasn't European enough to bow or kiss her fingers; I gave them an awkward American squeeze.

"Jack Squire," I said.

"If we are to be friends, Jack," Caterina said, "you must know that I always keep my promises."

"That's a good thing," I said, and we walked beneath the swaying lights down to Florian's, where the string trio was in its final flourish on the small stage outside. A thin crowd of late-night tourists stood watching the musicians flail away at "The Girl from Ipanema"; across the piazza, at the Caffè Veneziano, another trio answered with "That Old Devil Moon" performed by two violins and an accordion.

"It is not very good, this music," Caterina said, making a face. "Vivaldi himself played right where we are standing, with two hundred musicians all wearing green velvet. Ah! so beautiful!"

"You sound like you were there," I said.

"Vivaldi belongs to all Venetians of all times," she said.

"Do you want to go to Harry's Bar for a drink," I said. "Since it's just around the corner."

"Harry's closes at eleven o'clock," she said. "Besides it is much too expensive. Sixteen thousand lire for a gin-tonic? Ridiculous! I know a much better place."

The only sound was the hush of the oar in the still water of the canal. A few small lights showed in the blind backs of the buildings; the rest was blackness. No lantern hung from the ornamental prow. The gondolier was a gaunt young man wearing a black leather jacket over the traditional striped shirt. His straw hat was pulled low over his face and he was barefoot. He seemed to navigate by smell. At times, I couldn't make out Caterina sitting beside me on the thick cushions.

She lit a cigarette, and in the flare of the match I saw her black eyes staring into nothing.

"Cigarette?" she said. "These are French."

"Not right now," I said.

We sat in silence for a while and I listened to the dripping of the old buildings and the inscrutable silence of Venice at night.

"Doesn't he sing?" I said at last.

"Who?" Caterina said.

"The gondolier."

"Mercifully, no."

"What about you?"

She took a drag off her cigarette, and I thought I saw her smile.

"I sing to my cats," she said. "But so low only they can hear."

"Why don't you try me?"

She blew a cloud of cigarette smoke into the air over her shoulder and stubbed it out between her forefinger and thumb. I winced, but she did not seem to feel the pain.

"Very well, I will sing an old song," she said. "It is the song La Maddalena sang as she washed Christ's feet, as she dried them with her hair, repenting of her sins of the flesh, leaving her life as a whore behind forever."

When she sang, I felt it down in my toes. Her voice was low and supple. I closed my eyes for a moment and saw pale birds wheeling in the air, the little wavelets of the lagoon washing over mossy stones. The moment after the last note echoed against the dark walls of the buildings, I was prepared to believe whatever she would say next. Just then, my market watch went off, two long, two short. The shrill, insistent notes broke the mood entirely. It even seemed to throw the gondolier off his game; we bumped gently against a half-submerged piling in the gloom.

"What is that terrible noise?" Caterina said, annoyed.

"Excuse me, I've just got to check something," I said. I took the watch from my pocket, pressed the illuminated readout button, and peered into the tiny screen. *Fiat–Nissan deal collapses—lira falls against yen, brisk trading,*

Tokyo. Suddenly, I began to sweat. My ears popped. I realized now that I had forgotten to set my levels at the end of the day. I patted my pocket for my cellular phone, it wasn't there. I had left it on the marble shelf in the bathroom. Lack of sleep had made me dangerously careless. The three million made for the bank today would be lost again in the morning. This was a disaster.

"I've got to get to a phone," I said, trying to keep the desperation out of my voice. "Is there a phone around here?" The hollow echo of my words in the darkness told me this was a ridiculous question.

Caterina was silent for a beat. "I did not like to look at your face just then," she said quietly. "Your face was full of green light from that object." She pointed to the market watch. "It is a demon, you should throw it into the canal."

"We're talking about a lot of money here," I said, trying to calm myself. "Can you get me to a phone?"

"Public telephones in Venice are hard to find," she said. "And this part of the city is very old. There are phones in the cafes in the Piazza San Marco, but they will be closed now. Only in the train station, I think. But by gondola, it will take an hour. If we walk, still an hour."

An hour! I checked my watch again, tried to figure what time it was in Tokyo, in New York. The news was hitting now. In the great financial capitals, in Paris and Berlin, in Stockholm and Seoul, traders were putting the prices up on the big board. Millions were changing hands twice a second, everyone was selling lire, buying yen. At most, fifteen minutes was all you had.

"Never mind," I said in a trembling voice. "It's already too late."

"Then I am very sorry." Caterina took off her glove

and put her hand over mine. It was the first time we had really touched. Her skin was cool and smooth as a stone polished by the years. The anxiety seemed to drain out of me. I slumped back into the brocade cushions, exhausted.

"Would you like me to sing again?" she said, her lips no more than an inch from my ear.

"Yes," I said. "I would like that very much." Suddenly, I couldn't think of anything I would like better. Her voice rose again into the night, this time a Venetian lullaby, and I closed my eyes and again the soft images came: I saw white shapes in green water and shadows playing across the surface of the lagoon and then, in an instant, I was asleep.

10

WE WERE GLIDING THROUGH the water gate of a ruined palazzo. The first floor stood entirely flooded under a foot or two of water. A series of wooden planks resting on cinder blocks led through the gloom to a flight of slime-covered steps. The heavy air held the thick smell of old bones and mold.

"I'm sorry," I said, rubbing my face, "how long was I asleep?"

"Not long, just a few minutes," Caterina said. "Perhaps you were tired."

The gondolier steered the glossy barque to a makeshift mooring, and Caterina rose quickly and sprang up onto the wooden planks, and I saw that she was barefoot again.

"You must be careful along here," she said. "It is not

deep, the water, but you would ruin your nice shoes." She reached down and took my hand and led me along the planks. When I looked back over my shoulder, the gondolier was gone.

"Didn't you have to pay the man?" I said.

"He knows me," Caterina said. "He works for my father."

We mounted the stairs to the *piano nobile*, a single huge high-ceilinged room furnished with broken-down, ancient furniture. Xylophone music came from somewhere; I recognized the green reek of hash. A crowd of fifty or so people wreathed in smoke were gathered around a bar lit with candles at the far end. Large gothic windows overlooked an empty campo across the canal, alive with the vague shapes of cats in the darkness. The sibilant slur of the Venetian dialect hung in empty space beneath the ceiling like mist.

"This is a private club," Caterina whispered in my ear. "A friend of mine, he runs it to pay the taxes. His family has owned this palazzo for five hundred years, and he is too proud to accept aid from the government. You see those frescoes?"

I looked up and saw dark angels dancing in the vaulted recesses of the ceiling.

"They were painted by the great Tiepolo."

We made our way to the bar. A long-toothed, yellow-faced man served us two small glasses of a brownish liquid without being asked. His bony wrists protruded a good three inches from the end of his red jacket as he poured the stuff from a sticky bottle. I held up my drink to the yellow light of the candles; odd bits of sediment seemed to be floating just above the bottom of the glass. When I passed it under my nose, the bouquet was something between rubbing alcohol and burnt leather.

"What is this exactly?" I said.

"Teriaca," Caterina said. "My friend Tisi makes it himself. A very special drink. Good for your health. Only in Venice do you find this. *Chin-chin.*"

She knocked hers back in one gulp and I did the same. It burned on its way down and the kick was tremendous, went right to my head. The aftertaste was indescribable, a mixture of cinnamon, licorice, oranges, and something else. We drank two more in quick succession, then Caterina set about selecting the wine. The bartender brought several cobweb-covered bottles out from under the bar and wiped them down with a damp towel. She inspected them carefully, tapping each one with her fingernails, turning them upside down, brushing her nose against the seals of cracking red wax.

"Tisi keeps an excellent cellar," she said. "But one must be very careful. This bottle, for example, has turned." She handed one of the bottles back to the bartender with a few quick words. Unmoved, he cracked the neck open on the side of the ceramic sink behind the bar and poured the contents down the drain. For a moment the air was filled with the strong odor of vinegar.

I took this opportunity to get a good look at the other patrons. They were all done up in extravagant outdated evening wear: I saw white dinner jackets, bow ties, strapless dresses, cuff links, cigarette holders, spike heels. I even saw a pair of spats and a boa of green feathers. Their faces looked waxy in the candlelight, their eyes druggy and expressionless. I remembered a place like this in New York, a floating retro club called the Four Hundred, held in various abandoned warehouses in the meat market district a few years back. There had been a self-conscious air of the theatrical about that place, of hip kids playing dress-up. Not so, this crowd. The people here were older and seemed entirely at ease, as if they had been born in these clothes, as if they had just walked off the pages of *Town and County*, circa 1948.

Caterina picked her wine at last, a squat, dark bottle with a faded label, and she took two delicate fluted glasses and a corkscrew and motioned me through the crowd.

"Come, meet some of my friends," she said. I followed her over to a low couch near the windows, where a fat man and two women sat very close together, smoking hash from a small ebony pipe. The green reek again assaulted my nostrils. Suddenly, I could see tomorrow's headline flashing urgently on my market watch: *American FX trader caught in raid on Venice drug club. Dollar plummets.* But this was Europe, hash was practically legal, right?

The fat man wore a rumpled tuxedo with faint green stains along the sheeny collar. His head was almost the exact dimensions of a bowling ball, his fat feet stuffed into the smallest embroidered slippers imaginable. The women, both pale-skinned creatures with dyed red hair, wore matching dresses of complementary colors. They looked very stoned, the same witless grins plastered on their faces. The one on the right fanned herself vigorously with a painted ivory fan, despite the cool dampness of the evening.

"My friend is an American," Caterina announced to them in a loud voice. "As a courtesy, we will speak English."

"No, that's all right," I said quickly. "I understand a little Italian," but as I said this in English, the statement failed to have its intended effect. For a long moment, all three of them blinked up at us, like lost dogs.

"Welcome to my house," the fat man said at last. His

voice was gravelly and sounded like years of grappa and funny cigarettes. He struggled to get up, Caterina waved him down, and we took our place on a large carpet-covered ottoman directly across from them.

"I think you have smoked too much of that!" Caterina said to him. She pointed at the pipe and wrinkled her nose in disgust.

"We must have our pleasures," the fat man said, forming his words with exaggerated care. "How else are we to stand our special purgatory?"

"How you talk, Caterina, *cara!*" the redhead without the fan said, staring directly at me. "Since it seems you have grown tired of your cats!"

Caterina handed me the bottle of wine and corkscrew, and the four of them lapsed immediately into an argument in Italian. I had no idea what they were saying, but the fat man sounded upset about something. Then, Caterina made a sharp comment and the fat man grunted and extinguished the ebony hash pipe by placing his thumb over the burning embers in the bowl. Feeling out of place, I concentrated on opening the wine. I cut around the wax seal carefully. The cork was black with age. The label on the bottle was old and yellow and handwritten in a faint, flowery script. I couldn't make out the year, which had been rubbed clean. After some effort, the cork came out with a dry pop and I filled the glasses. Caterina took her glass from me and smiled.

"To our friendship," she said, and I saw the light of the candles reflected in her black eyes.

"I'll drink to that." The wine was fruity and resinous. I had never tasted anything quite like it. "Very good," I said.

"You like it?" The fat man leaned forward. "Tokay. My father brought over several cases many years ago. Out of fashion now, the sweet wines of the past. Drier wines are preferred these days, I should think."

"Excuse me for not making proper introductions," Caterina said, lowering her glass. "This is Tisiano Naso. Tisi, this is my friend Jack Squire."

I reached across and shook his hand, which felt like a dead fish.

"And these are Bianca and Angela."

I smiled and nodded at the two redheads, not sure which was which. One smiled back, the other giggled stupidly from behind her fan.

"So you live here?" I said to the fat man.

He flashed a humorless smile. "Oh, not anymore," he said. "Not for more than two hundred years."

"What Tisi means," the redhead without the fan said, "is this was the house of his family, yes? They were in the *Libro d'Oro*, yes?"

The fat man rolled his eyes. "Please," he said. "All that is finished."

"No, not finished," the redhead with the fan said, giggling. "Tisi, N.H.," forming the letters in the air with her finger. *"Nobile Homine.* Count Tisi, eh?"

I nodded, though I didn't know what the hell they were talking about.

"The *Libro d'Oro*, this is the Golden Book of Venice," Caterina said, turning to me. "Once, many years ago, in the days of La Serenissima—that is the old Venetian Republic—every person of noble family was inscribed in the Golden Book. It was a big book with gold covers kept in the Doge's Palace. If your name was not in the Golden Book, you were nothing. Peasants, fishermen, sheep to be led. Tisi's family was in the Golden Book, as was mine, and Bianca's and Angela's too. Once we were all very high, now we are nothing, we are Barnabotti."

"Barnabotti?" I said. "What is that?"

Caterina hesitated. "Is difficult to explain," she said. "And Tisi is right. Today, in modern times, all of it means nothing."

"Yes, exactly zero," the fat man said, with some satisfaction. "Are we better than other people? No," he shook his jowly face. "Were we better than other people in those days?" He shrugged.

All of this was beyond me. I didn't know what to say. For a beat I could almost hear the sound of the water eating away at the foundations of the palazzo, a slow creaking like the walls giving way.

"Have you ever thought of reclaiming the first floor?" I said awkwardly at last. "Pumping out the water, shoring it up? A team of engineers could work wonders with this place."

Tisi raised an eyebrow, his waxy jowls sagging. I had to repeat myself three times before he understood, the idea seemed so outlandish to him.

"You mean to save Venice?" he said at last.

"I suppose that's the bigger picture," I said.

"But it is already beyond the work of men, of machines," he said. "Venice has already sunk. It is gone. Most of the pilings beneath the palazzos are over a thousand years old. Many have rotted away, and many more will rot soon. Venice is floating on air, it is an illusion, a mirage, a lost city. Or we might say it is a miracle, that there's a hand that sustains her from above. An army of angels with chains of gold that keeps her up. Of course, even angels grow weary, fall by the wayside."

"Oh, you are a great poet, Tisi," the redhead without the fan said. The sneer in her voice made it an insult. "The American talks of engineers and you talk of angels. He will take you for a fool."

"And you for a stupid little slut!" the fat man said between his teeth, and the two of them began to spit at each other in their own language.

Caterina sighed and turned to me. "Would you like to dance?"

I looked around. There was no one else dancing. "Looks kind of lonely out there," I said.

"We will dance," she said.

"I don't really know how," I said, embarrassed.

"Come with me," she said.

At the center of the room, there was a smooth square of polished marble not much bigger than a dining room table. We stood on this and swayed in each other's arms to the vague music of the xylophone. I could feel the hard contours of her body beneath her dress. Her skin had taken on a slight chill. Her hair smelled like damp flowers at a funeral.

"I'm afraid my friends, they do not . . ." She let her voice trail off and she reached up and put her cold hand on the back of my neck. "No. Let us not talk now. Let us be very quiet."

"O.K.," I said.

We danced like that for a long time, that is, hardly dancing at all, and not saying a word. The impermanent gray of a false dawn showed beyond the gothic curves of the windows. It was three a.m., the hour of wakefulness; cats roamed the empty campo below, looking for their dinner. Slowly, known to us all, yet imperceptible, Venice was sinking into the muck of the lagoon.

11

RINIO WENT TO PADUA on bank business for a week and I had the office to myself. I closed the door, shut down the board, turned off the trading screens, and told Vida to hold all calls not from the United States. My first report on the Italian political scene was due in Warren's office on Tuesday next, and I hadn't even begun my research. Warren wanted more than the straight news, more than Reuters or UPI could provide, he wanted the vibe on the street. The problem with Venice was that the streets were full of water and no one I knew seemed to care about politics.

"Venice is part of Italy only because of economic reasons," Rinio had said before he left. "If it was possible to bring back the Serenissima without going bankrupt, no true Venetian would oppose the change. Here, we are Venetians first and Italians second. Politics is something that happens on Terra Firma."

This attitude was shared by Vida and the desk clerk at the hotel, by the old man who shined shoes in the lobby of the Comparini Bank, by the girl behind the counter of the wine bar in the Campo Santa Maria Formosa who was a student in political science taking a semester off from the university in Bologna.

"You must understand, signore," the girl said, "Italy has experienced fifty-five different governments since 1945. One government more or less . . ." She gave an Italian shrug.

When the wine bar closed, I offered her a coffee at the little espresso place next door. We sat at an outside table and watched the night sky fade and become indistinct

with haze, the store owners pull down their metal shutters against the few tourists still strolling about at the late
hour of ten o'clock. The austere neoclassical facade of
Santa Maria Formosa went thick with shadows across the
way. After a while, a gang of youths accompanied by a
large dog came to play soccer in the vacant campo. The
old stones rang with their shouts, the barking of the dog
and the dull thud of the ball against shoe leather.

The girl's name was Paolina, she was twenty-one,
unattractive, and intelligent enough to be unhappy with
her lot in life. She had no interest in politics, it turned
out. Her abiding passion seemed to be for American rock
and roll.

"You know this group, they are called Ahrem?" she
said over the second cup of espresso.

I shook my head.

"It is three letters," she said, tracing them on the tablecloth.

"Oh, R.E.M.," I said. "Yes, of course."

"You like?"

"Sure."

"In Bologna, at the university, very easy to find sympathetic people. They like the new music, they like the new
things. Here . . ." She gestured at the youths in the
campo now playing shirts and skins. A dozen bare backs
glistened with sweat in the light of the streetlamp. The
dog, a half-blind shaggy creature, ran in and out between
them, getting in the way of the ball, tripping up the play-
ers as they took a shot for the goal.

"I play the harmonica," she said suddenly. "Perhaps
you would like to hear sometime?"

I tried to steer her back to the elections in April. I
asked questions about Berlusconi, the incumbent prime
minister, about Prodi, his opponent.

"Berlusconi, this man is an actor, not a politician," she said. "Everyone knows this. He comes to interviews already with his makeup on and lets the camera photograph him only from certain angles, so he looks good on the television. Also, they say he has many mistresses. They say he sleeps with a different woman every night. And they say he is a fascist. Yes, this is what they say. Prodi, he is new face. Never in politics before. A good man, maybe." She couldn't tell me anything else.

"But I thought you were a student of political science," I said.

She nodded, her eyes a little sad. "Yes, yes I am," she said. "But I am more interested in the music. Politics, you know, they change every year. But music . . ." She brightened a little. "Music is for always. Everyone, they still listen to Rossini, Vivaldi, yes? The politicians, who remembers?"

In the end, I downloaded two years' worth of the *The Washington Post* from the Internet onto my computer and tried to write my report from that. The *Post's* foreign service had done a series of articles on the Italian political scene starting with the elections in March 1994. The situation in Italy was complicated and chaotic: near as I could figure it, in the early nineties a series of bribery scandals had destroyed the ruling coalition of Christian Democrats who had dominated Italian politics for almost forty years. By January 1994, half the leaders of the old guard were under indictment for corruption, including the former prime minister, Bettino Craxi; the other half were already in jail.

Into this mess strode media tycoon Silvio Berlusconi. He was a flamboyant character, the Citizen Kane–esque owner of Italy's three large television networks whose programming consisted largely of American TV shows dubbed in Italian and variety hours in which big-breasted women took off their clothes before appreciative audiences. Berlusconi formed a new right-wing party called Forza Italia with political rivals Gianfranco Fini of the neofascist National Alliance and Umberto Bossi of the separatist Northern League. This unlikely coalition, aided by hundreds of hours of free pro-Forza TV advertising on Berlusconi's stations, swept the March '94 national elections.

But Forza's triumph was short-lived. Fini favored a strong national government in the tradition of Mussolini; Bossi, a federated state with more autonomy for the regions and less tax money for the impoverished south; Berlusconi stood everywhere and nowhere, somewhere in between the two, a man with no fixed agenda except power. Thus, opposing tensions in the party caused the government to collapse in December after less than seven months in Rome. A nonelected caretaker government under technocrat Lamberto Dini took over the day-to-day details of running the country, and would step down after the next round of national elections.

Meanwhile in June, the Italian people had been forced to vote on twelve referendums concerning matters usually handled by an elected parliament. Among other issues, they voted on the number of hours grocery stores could stay open, the number of television stations any person could own at once, whether movies on television could be interrupted by commercials. Ballots were color-coded, sometimes yes meant no, the confusion was general. This episode of legislative chaos gave Italian parties of the left impetus to regroup. Romano Prodi, a mild-mannered professor of economics, managed to put together a coalition of former communists and socialists into a party called L'Ulivo, the Olive Tree, which quickly picked up a surprising amount of popular support.

In April, candidates for the Olive Tree will stand against Berlusconi and his new Freedom Alliance Party, hammered together out of the remaining pieces of Forza Italia. Speculation in the press was contradictory. No one could say which way the elections would turn. The polls were unreliable; both parties were racked with dissent, as always. People hated Berlusconi or loved him, Prodi had all the charisma of a wet linguini, the columnists said. Olive Tree would be forced to rely on the support of hard-line Marxists of the Refoundation Party who had refused to admit communism was dead; Freedom Alliance would once again turn to the fascists of the far right, including Alessandra Mussolini, granddaughter of the famous dictator, who was already an elected representative for Naples. Every Italian wanted politics that did not call attention to itself, a two-party system, regular elections, trains that ran on time, a manageable national debt, lower unemployment, prime ministers who could actually do something—but no one knew how to get there. As of now, the elections were anyone's game.

I read through the material twice, made careful notes over five sheets of a legal pad, then broke my pencil in half and stared at a fly crawling across the ceiling. I had no interest in this situation at all. I was not a political analyst, I was a trader in world currencies, and despite my education, not a man given to subtlety. And I couldn't get Caterina's face out of my mind.

She was a strange, ethereal woman who would not trust me with her phone number or address. She lived with her father, she said; he was very strict and did not like men calling the house. So we made dates always at midnight, to meet in the Piazza San Marco under the big clock, in this or that campo, on the steps of this or that church, on the Rialto bridge, before the main door of the Ca' Rezzonico. She was always where she said she would be, never more than a few minutes late. We saw each other only a brief hour or two over a glass of wine before she went off on her self-appointed crusade to feed the cats of the city.

I barely slept these days, just a few winks between three and seven a.m., by which time the Grand Canal below my window was a blaze of terrible, glorious light. I had reached a curious state beyond exhaustion where the mundane objects of life seemed hyperreal, full of vibrant color; where the gray skies on cloudy days glowed with an intense, violent illumination. Even the cursor on my trading screen, that dim electronic blip bouncing between lira, dollar, and yen, burned my eyes. I wore dark sunglasses everywhere, even along the narrow streets at dusk. We hadn't kissed, we rarely touched more than shaking hands. Still, I couldn't get Caterina's face out of my mind.

12

A FLAT, HAZY LIGHT FILLED the sky over the lagoon. The sun stood bright at eleven in the morning, partially obscured by a bank of high, magnificent clouds. In the far distance, the faint peaks of the Dolomites could be made out against the blue. Closer off the port bow, Burano's campanile leaned rakishly above the horizon at an angle of sixty-five degrees. Gulls and white-bellied swallows wheeled overhead. At the controls of the Arkansas Traveller, Rinio looked the very picture of the well-dressed yachtsman. He wore an ascot of red and yellow silk folded carefully into his white shirt and a red carnation stuck through the gold band of his captain's hat. He held a large glass of Campari and soda in one hand; the other rested lightly on the wheel.

"So, have you made love with her?" he said.

I thought about not answering, then I shrugged. "No," I said.

"And how many times have you been out together?"

"Four times . . . no, five. Five times."

He slapped the wheel and the Arkansas Traveller lurched a little to the starboard. "Giacomo, Giacomo!" It was what he called me now that we were friends. "You must realize this is an Italian woman, yes?"

I nodded. "Venetian, actually," I said.

"Good, very good . . . but you miss the point. With an Italian woman, especially with a Venetian woman, you must be very firm. You must be like a man. You want her body? You don't tell her, you don't ask her, you take it! *Capisci?*"

I thought this over for a minute. "I'm not sure if I want her body," I said. "I mean I do and I don't. She's sort of strange."

Rinio wrinkled up his forehead and stuck out his lower lip. "I do not understand," he said. "She is attractive, yes?"

"Yes and no," I said. "She's very unusual-looking."

"Giacomo! You are being very difficult!"

"You've got to realize I'm coming down from a two-and-a-half-year relationship . . ." I began, but Rinio waved me off.

"My friend, answer me this," he said. "Do you think

about her all the time? Do you feel her all the time right here?" He put a hand like a claw over his heart.

"I think about her a lot," I said quietly.

"Ah! You see!" he said, and made a gesture that included the horizon. "Love!"

"Not quite." I smiled. "I hardly know her."

"What is her name, maybe I know her," he smirked. "Venice is not very large place, you see."

I hesitated. The thought that Rinio might have slept with Caterina caused a sudden clenching in my bowels. "Her name is Caterina," I said. "Caterina Vendramin."

"Vendramin?" Rinio made a face that meant he was suitably impressed. "This is a very old Venetian name. Very old, very fine. One of the early doges, he had this name, but I did not know . . ." He paused and shook his head.

"What?"

"I did not know there were any Vendramins left in Venice. I read in books, in school that the family is extinct."

"This one's not extinct," I said. "And she's got a father who won't let her out of the house."

"They have all got fathers," he said. "And uncles and brothers also. Don't let that stop you!"

And we both laughed.

We went to Cipriani's, on Torcello, open for the last days of the season, and sat under the grape arbor along the canal lined with glossy speedboats. The terrace was crowded with wealthy Italians and their mistresses. Stocky, middle-aged businessmen in expensive silk sport jackets entertained tables full of young women wearing revealing sundresses. It was that sort of place.

"You like octopussy?" the waitress asked, hearing us speak English.

"Yes," I said. "I like octopussy very much."

Rinio ordered for both of us: a thin, flavorful shellfish soup, linguini colored with squid ink and topped with a light tomato-garlic sauce, and the octopus itself, head, tentacles, and all, served in a thick paste of its own ink— washed down with two bottles of crisp white wine from the Veneto. Everything was excellent. In the green shade under the grape arbor, with a good meal in my stomach and slightly tipsy, I didn't feel tired at all, I felt fine. American jazz floated out to us from the bar.

"Your American writer Hemingway came to this restaurant very often," Rinio said.

"I can see that he would like it here," I said, looking around.

"Of course, that was many years ago. Cipriani's in Hemingway's time, you know, it was a very private place. Now, it is full of tourists."

"Today?" I raised an eyebrow. "Everyone here looks Italian to me."

"Oh yes, today is the end of the season," he said. "Few tourists, so the Italians they come. But I am also thinking of Venice, you see. In my city during the summer, the tourists, they are more than the inhabitants by two to one. We cannot afford to live in our own city anymore. Rich foreigners, and I mean even other Italians, from Milan, from Turin or Rome, they buy palazzos on the Grand Canal and spend one or two weeks in spring, maybe a month in summer. And so the rents go up and there becomes no place for us Venetians to live. The real Venice, you ask, where is it?" He gave an expressive shrug. "The islands of the Rialto, they are more and more like your Disneyland, just for the tourists, eh? Perhaps the real Venice is now on Terra Firma, in Mestre, in Chioggia. In these places, there are poor people, and middle-class, they work, they have homes. It is sad, because Mestre is an ugly place. Many refineries, chemical factories. The air it smells so bad."

After lunch, we moved into the bar for a *digestif*. The barman, a friend of Rinio's cousin from Burano, set two tiny liqueur glasses and a round bottle of Unicom down on the counter, with a gesture that meant take as much as you like. The stuff was bitter and thick as paint. It had all the bite of the Teriaca I'd had with Caterina with none of the rich aftertaste.

"What was it you drank, Giacomo?" Rinio said, raising an eyebrow.

"It was called Teriaca," I said. "Like this, only better. Very good, actually."

Rinio shook his head. "Teriaca, it is not a liqueur," he said. "It is old-fashioned medicine. Many, many years ago, the people took it against the plague. Of course, it never worked. One time in the Cinquecento, fifty thousand people died in Venice, one hundred thousand in the lagoon. This Teriaca did not work for them. Still the Venetians took it for everything, for the stomach, the liver, the heart. My grandfather he drank it every night, like wine. But, now the government say it is not legal to make Teriaca anymore, because they put in the opium and a few other things the government does not like."

Opium. It figured. I still couldn't remember how I'd gotten home that night. I brooded on the decadent habits of Caterina's friends as Rinio continued with his chosen subject. The man had a one-track mind, by which I mean, among other things, that he could only deal with one subject at a time.

"But what must be done about our poor Venice?" Rinio said now, starting into his third glass of Unicom. "This is a question that confuses everyone. There must be a way for the real people to live and work in the city. I ask you, what is our city without the people who built it from the lagoon? It ceases to exist, it is like a museum or an amusement park. I say Venice for the Venetians first, then the tourists second! Last year the mayor . . ."

I stopped listening and found myself wondering what Caterina was doing now. I tried, but could not imagine her by daylight. A warm breeze ruffled the surface of the canal. A group of blond German tourists moved stiffly up the brick path that led out to the vaporetto landing. The campanile of Santa Maria dell'Assunta cast its long shadow over small fields of eggplants and onions, separated by low hedges. Once, six or seven centuries ago, this island had been as densely populated as Venice itself, home to twenty thousand people—this fact recalled from the *Michelin Green Guide to Venice*. Now, it was a pleasant backwater of vegetable fields and reeds, home to Cipriani's, a handful of market gardeners, and the ancient brick cathedral. In A.D. 421, so the story goes, the earliest refugees came to Torcello from the mainland, fleeing invading Visigoths. The first Venetians were led across the waste of marshes by a Christian bishop and a flock of holy doves. In those days, the air itself must have been thick with miracles.

As Rinio finished his Unicom, two young Italian women in transparent white dresses came in to sit at the end of the bar. They were pretty, with black hair and greenish eyes, so alike they could have been sisters. Gold jewelry showed the color of butter against their tanned skin. You could see their dark nipples through the sheer fabric of their dresses. Rinio put his glass down and stared. One of them looked back, a frank evaluating gaze, then looked slowly away. Rinio elbowed me excitedly.

"You see that? They are for us, my friend," he whispered in my ear.

"What about your wife?" I whispered back.

He grinned, showing his teeth. "Today, my wife is not here. Today, I am a bachelor."

We moved down to the end of the bar a minute later, and Rinio immediately struck up a conversation. Neither of the young women spoke English, and I wasn't in the mood for sign language. I left Rinio engaged in an animated discussion with both of them, and walked up the dusty path to the cathedral, past old ladies selling lace tablecloths and placemats, and lazy cats sprawled in the shade of gnarled olive trees. Inside the cathedral, it was cold and gloomy and crumbling, like every other church in Italy, and there was the familiar smell of mold and old bones. But the famous mosaics in the transept glowed bright as the day they were made: the golden panels showed saints and demons and naked sinners suffering the fires of hell, and piles of skulls with worms threading in and out of the eye sockets. I stared up at these last two panels for some time, hands in my pocket, a curious sensation of déjà-vu wrinkling across my skin.

13

SIGNOR EMILIO ZATTARE, one of the senior vice presidents of the Comparini Bank, flew in from Milan on Tuesday, and all day the building was in an uproar. Secretaries scurried down the corridors, their arms full of papers, telephones rang and kept ringing, waiters in short white jackets strutted in and out of the boardroom with trays of prosciutto and cheese hardrolls and pitchers of coffee, and even Rinio seemed a little flustered. He wore his best suit, a very tasteful, very expensive dark blue number designed by Francesco Ferre, and tried to look busy whenever he heard footsteps passing our office door, which he kept propped open so people could see we were working inside.

At last, Carlo Orti, the manager of regional affairs, came in and sat importantly in the swivel chair across from our desks. Because of the visit of Signor Zattare from Milan, he said, the entire bank staff was being invited to La Fenice the next evening for a performance of Mozart's *Don Giovanni*. Then he handed over the tickets, carefully wrapped in a square of blue tissue paper as if they were unusually fragile pieces of Murano glass.

"Take my ticket and give it to your wife," I said to Rinio, when Carlo was gone. "I hate opera. In any case, I'm supposed to meet my friend tomorrow tonight."

Rinio stepped around and put a serious hand on my shoulder. "No, Giacomo," he said. "This is more important than any woman. This is *business*. When Signor Zattare invites you to the opera, you go to the opera."

Our seats were in a far corner of the upper tier, our view of the stage, half obscured by a gilded column. Signor Zattare himself sat enthroned below in the box reserved in former days for the doges of Venice, directly overlooking the action. I caught a glimpse of him in the lobby during the entr'acte, surrounded by sycophants, a silver-haired gentleman with the dignified aspect of Victor Emmanuel, Italy's last king, accompanied by a busty blond woman in furs who looked like a trashy starlet and was most probably his wife.

I dozed off and on through the first hour, slept soundly

through the second, waking with a start in time to see the statue of the Commander come to life and drag the hapless Don Giovanni down to hell through a trapdoor out of which crepe paper flames blew in the wind from a concealed fan. I looked at my watch, and felt panic grip my gut. It was a quarter past midnight. I had meant to leave half an act early, so as to keep my date with Caterina in the Piazza San Marco.

I got up and hurried out before the final curtain call, but arrived forty-five minutes late in front of Florian's, our usual spot. The piazza was nearly deserted, waiters moved between the tables, stacking the chairs. I waited another half hour, my heart filling with something very much like despair. My connection to Caterina was so tenuous, we were held together by the barest thread. With no phone number, no address, and no way to reach her, one missed meeting might mean we would never see each other again. Maybe she was married—the thought struck me like an electric shock. Yes, she was probably married, there might even be kids. I trailed up the Calle dei Fabbri turning this scenario over in my mind. I didn't want to imagine Caterina sharing another man's bed, couldn't imagine her as a mother, but it was possible. Maybe it was best that I did not see her again. Maybe it was best. . . .

"Jack . . ."

I jumped. Caterina stepped out of the shadows of the Campo San Benedetto, just around the corner from my hotel. The wind off the lagoon was quite chilly tonight; she wore her black domino pulled closed, hood up around her face.

"I remember you said you lived at the the Palazzo Bragadino," she said. "They said you were not in, that they did not know where—" She stopped herself and looked me up and down. I had rented a tuxedo for the opera at Rinio's insistence. "You have been to La Fenice," she said.

"How did you know?" I said.

"Where else is there to go in Venice at night, dressed like that?"

"It was a work thing," I said. "I couldn't get out of it. I would have called to tell you, but then again I don't have your phone number."

"My father . . ." She hesitated. "You see, we do not have a telephone."

"Caterina, are you married?" I tried to find her black eyes in the shadows beneath the hood.

She looked away. For a moment, all Venice was still. Over her shoulder, down the narrow alley fronting the hotel, I saw the red lights of a police boat reflected off the black waters of the Grand Canal. Then, she stepped up to me and put the palm of her hand against my face. It felt cool and dry and sent a little shock up my spine.

"I would like to see your rooms," she said. "Where you live. Do you mind?"

Caterina wandered through the apartment, picking up familiar objects—a spoon, my electric razor, a plastic photo cube brought from my collection at home—and examining them as if they were exotic treasures from a thieves' cave in the *Arabian Nights*. She went into the bathroom and tried the faucets, looked into the medicine cabinet for a good five minutes, handling the bottles of aspirin and antihistamine, the tubes of cortisone and toothpaste, then she went into the bedroom and bounced up and down on the unmade bed like a customer testing a mattress in a furniture store. After a moment, she picked a beige plastic object out of the tangled sheets. It was oval, about as large as an ostrich egg, and fitted with a blue dial and five blue buttons.

"I just had that sent from home," I said from the doorway. "Ordered it out of the Sharper Image catalogue."

"Come?"

"Never mind. You want to see what it does, press one of the buttons."

She held it between her fingers, unsure of herself.

"Go ahead."

She pressed one of the blue buttons. The machine came to life with a dull electronic hushing and she gave a little shriek and threw it back into the sheets.

"You're listening to Big Sur," I said, laughing. "That's a sleep machine. It makes sounds to help you sleep. Here . . ." I sat beside her and demonstrated the other choices. There was Jungle Rain, Babbling Brook, October Night, and Willow Wind—all of which sounded much the same, like a fan going in a wind tunnel.

Caterina frowned. "Do you like this?"

"No," I said.

"Does it help you sleep?"

"Not really."

She had yet to remove her domino. She jumped up suddenly and swung it from her shoulders, and I saw she was wearing just the right amount of nothing at all: a low-cut, very short black dress, the bodice held up by thin spaghetti straps fastened with tiny scallop-shell clasps. Her shoulders gleamed in the white light of the overhead. Her feet were bare. They looked cold against the dull marble of the floor.

"Isn't it a little chilly to be going around still barefoot?" I said.

Caterina ignored this question and went back into the living room and picked up the photo cube again and turned it over slowly, this time studying each surface: there was a photo of Mom standing hands clasped, dour as a nun, before the swing set in the backyard of our old bungalow in Shirlington; a photo of Father at the Pentagon smiling grimly the day of his promotion to full-bird colonel; a photo of Elizabeth as a kitten curled up in a basket of clean clothes, a photo of myself at twelve years old on the parade ground in the tight dress grays and high plumed shako of St. Albert's Academy. The remaining two sides were taken up with commercial postcards of the prairie around Lincoln—yellow fields of wheat bending in the wind, the sky above blue as a cornflower and big as the whole world. I had a dozen such cubes full of photographs at home in a bookshelf in the condo in Arlington Mews. This was the childhood cube. On a long trip one must always take a few reminders of home, but just now I couldn't say why I had brought this one along.

"You are from a family of soldiers," Caterina said, pursing her lips.

"Just my father," I said. "I flunked out of military school in the tenth grade. He was infantry, World War II, got a field commission, then Korea and Vietnam. A career man."

"This is your mother?"

"Yes."

"She looks *triste*."

"She and my father weren't getting along too well back then," I said. "If she had lived, I think they might have gotten divorced. But she died not too long after that picture was taken. When I was a kid."

"Yes, I knew that."

"How?" I was surprised.

"It is in your face," Caterina said, and she raised her dark eyes to me. "You have the look of an orphan, like everyone has abandoned you. Your father, he is dead also?"

"No, my father is very much alive," I said. "He's a bastard, but he's still alive."

Caterina frowned and turned the cube over again. Her eyes lit up and she tapped her fingernail against the postcard of the prairie.

"Ah! This is your home?" she said.

"Not really," I said. "Just a place where I went to school."

She peered at it closely. "Very beautiful! What is it called?"

"They call it Nebraska," I said.

"Is it close by the sea?"

I smiled. "The nearest sea is about fifteen hundred miles away. There are a few ponds, but very small and full of catfish."

She looked puzzled. *"Non capisco."*

"Fish with long whiskers like a cat's," I said. "Sometimes, during rainstorms, they come out of the water and cross the road. You've got to be careful when you're driving."

Caterina stared at me for a moment, incredulous. Then she put her hand over her mouth and began to laugh. She rarely laughed, and the sound was startling, beautiful, clear as a bell. "Oh, you make up stories with me," she said. "Catfish? You are very funny!"

"Have it your own way," I said, smiling.

A few minutes later, done poking around, Caterina went into the bathroom. I heard the light splash of running water. She did not close the door completely, and from where I was sitting in the living room, I could see her washing her feet in the bidet. She soaped them with both hands, washed them off, then soaped them again. The water in the bowl was black. I felt like a stranger in my own apartment; somehow in the space of a quarter of an hour, she had made the place her own. I picked up the latest copy of *The Economist* from the coffee table and flipped through it. There was a long piece about the growing U.S. trade deficit with South Korea, another longer piece about brand-name counterfeiting in China. Interesting stuff as far as the currency market was concerned, but just now, I couldn't care less.

When Caterina came out of the bathroom again, she was naked, her dress and panties bunched up in one hand. She didn't say a word. I stared as she walked calmly into the bedroom. For a moment, I didn't know what to do. Then I put down the magazine and followed to the doorway. She had already settled into the sheets. I took a step toward the bed but she held up her hand.

"Please turn off the electric lights," she said.

I turned off the overhead from the switch on the wall. Her bare flesh shone a faint silver in the reflection of the lights outside along the Grand Canal. Her nipples looked like large black beetles clinging to the ends of her small breasts.

"This is not something I do with everyone," she said.

"Of course," I said.

"And you must not ask me for more than I can give. I have already given too much."

I didn't know what to make of this comment. I put it down to the residual Catholicism of Italian women: different currencies, I told myself, I'll deal with the exchange rate later. I gave an assenting grunt and dropped my trousers to the floor. The belt buckle made a small clanking sound against the marble tiles. I was already hard. When I knelt on the bed and put my arms around her, she felt cold as stone, and I thought for a quick, strange moment of grave markers and tombs before she began to warm beneath my touch.

14

RINIO AND I PUSHED OUR way through the lunchtime crowds to the Caffè Cagliostro, a Venetian-style sandwich shop across the canal from the bank. Venice is not a city of heavy daylight eaters; the better restaurants don't even open until eight-thirty in the evening. For lunch, most Venetians grab a quick cup of espresso and a couple of the small sandwiches that resemble hors d'oeuvres at a bad cocktail party. They are made of spongy, crustless white bread, cut into sailboat wedges, slathered with mayonnaise, and filled with a mayonnaisey paste of hard-boiled egg, onion, and shrimp, or egg and asparagus and onion, or any number of similar combinations of egg and other ingredients, the binding medium always being mayonnaise.

Rinio ordered a plate of ten of these disgusting little sandwiches, found a place at the counter against the window with a good view of the passing crowds, and began stuffing the wedges into his face two at a time. He would grunt whenever an attractive woman came down the street outside, reserving two grunts for a nice ass, a mayonnaise-smeared leer for large breasts jiggling under tight clothing. The effect was more comical than he knew. It was all I could do to keep myself from laughing out loud.

I drank two cups of espresso, ate half a *biscotto* and stared up at the square of clear blue sky visible above the roofs of the ancient buildings. There was a cold, thrilling smell in the air this morning that meant winter was coming. I pictured the far peaks of the Dolomites white with snow, clean fields of powder as white as Caterina's flesh, then I thought of making love to her again and felt a pleasant stirring between my legs.

I came back to myself a moment later, just as Rinio wagged a half-eaten wedge of sandwich in my face. He tried to speak, but his words came out a garble of egg, shrimp, and mayonnaise.

"Chew first, Rinio, then swallow."

He chewed and swallowed and cleared his throat. "There is something different about you today, Giacomo," he said. He wiped the mayonnaise from his face and studied me for a long moment. "Yes, there is something different. What is it, I ask myself?"

I could feel my ears turning red. "I don't know what you're talking about," I said, but I could not meet his eyes. There was a tightness of muscles at the back of my thighs that reminded me of Caterina.

"You look"—Rinio waved the sandwich wedge again and a chunk of pink shrimp fell onto his shoe—"you look—what is the American expression?—like the cat who has just come from eating the parrot."

"The canary."

"Sì, the canary." Then he paused and slapped the counter. "I know! It is that Vendramin woman, am I right? You have had sex with her!"

It was an uncanny bit of guesswork. I shook my head, but I couldn't keep the smile off my face.

"Ah, I knew it!" Rinio said. "It is true, yes?"

"That's none of your business," I said, still smiling.

But Rinio would not be denied. He was persistent and shameless and at last, back at the office after lunch, I gave up most of the story, omitting certain intimate details. He leaned back in his desk chair, the leather creaking, listening carefully. The insight of a born seducer regarding women cannot be underestimated; his knowledge of sexual matters was encyclopedic and untainted by any moral considerations.

"Still, you do not know where she lives, you know nothing about her," he said when I was finished.

"That's right," I said.

"You want my opinion?"

"Not really."

"I will give it anyway—you must understand that this woman not only has a father, she must also have a husband. A jealous husband."

"You can't say that for sure."

"No, but I am very familiar with the ways of Venetian women, you grant me this knowledge?"

"I grant you that knowledge."

"And I think your Vendramin, she is hiding something very serious. You must be careful of Venetian women, Giacomo. I cannot make this clear enough. Venetian women are very secretive, very dangerous. My wife, she is attractive, a good woman, you agree, yes?"

"Of course."

"Then why, you ask me, do I have so many girlfriends? This is the reason—I cheat on my wife because if I did not, she would cheat on me."

I thought it best not to question the logic of this statement. "Time to get back to work," I said, "the international currency market is a speeding train that waits for no man," but Rinio was not through with me.

"Come on, tell me one more thing." He leaned over his desk, his voice descending to a lascivious whisper.

"How is the sex with your Vendramin? Is it very hot? Does she—"

I cut him off right there, annoyed with myself for allowing our conversation to get this far. "Don't push your luck, Rinio," I said, and turned back to my trading screen, alight with numbers and arrows that represented, in faint luminescent shorthand, billions changing hands and changing back again.

Caterina's favorite position was something she called the *vongnole*: She would arrange herself facedown at the edge of the mattress, draw her knees to her breasts, push her rump in the air and expose her neat pudendum, pink as a clam in its shell of flesh. Sometimes, I would run my hands over the contours of her body for a good fifteen minutes before broaching anything more serious. She would sigh and murmur, blush charmingly beneath my touch. Her body was without blemish, oddly pale and smooth as polished marble. Up close, I could barely make out a single pore or hair. Finally I would take her hipbones in a firm grip and enter her standing, from behind. She would moan, cry out, call on God in her own soft language, pitch and buck against me, claw the sheets.

But beyond the *vongnole* and one or two other interesting positions, she was delightfully uninventive in bed. She would not indulge in the exotic activities that Cynthia or any other American woman I had been with took as a matter of course: today in America there is no sex that has not been tainted in some way by pornography, which is to say, by advertising. Women will perform certain sexual acts—give blow jobs, demand to be tied up and spanked, take it up the ass, whatever—not because these acts come naturally, but because everyone has read about them in *Cosmopolitan* or the *Penthouse* Forum, seen them acted out in X-rated flicks on the *Playboy* channel, heard Dr. So-and-So the famous sex therapist discuss the necessary components of a full and active sex life on talk radio.

Caterina did not indulge in any of this modern nonsense. For her, sex was not a matter for the public forum or scholarly debate, not a tool for empowering women after centuries of male dominance—none of that political claptrap. She made love like she had never seen a picture of anyone else making love. For her, sex was an echo in the darkness, the faint whispering of two souls each to each, separated by the barest membrane of flesh.

15

WARREN'S VOICE ROSE TO A metallic whine over the static of two continents, then the line went dead. The second broken connection in five minutes. I buzzed Vida on the intercom.

"Let's try it again," I said. "Third time's a charm."

It took three more attempts to establish a clear connection. Warren sounded irritated on the other end of the line. I imagined the sunlight streaming into his office through the blinds, the view of Lafayette Park and the White House behind its new concrete barricades on the other side of Pennsylvania Avenue.

"I've got a meeting at three-thirty, Jack," he said.

"Sorry," I said. "Italian telephones. Venice is farther away than you think."

"I'm going to have to cut to the chase," he said. "I'm conferencing in Candace Searles. You know Candace?"

"Yes, of course," I said. "We met at the CMVC convention in Chicago last year." I remembered a short, hard-boiled woman with thick round glasses and enormous breasts. A top-notch trader. She had no husband or children and was married to her job in the way nuns were married to Christ—a platonic, all-encompassing relationship, but emphatically nonorgasmic.

"We're moving her up to the chief trading spot out there, and I wanted her to listen in on this."

"Glad to have her input!" I said, my heart sinking. This was an uncomfortable surprise. One of Warren's little managerial tricks to test his subordinate's agility under stress.

"Hello Jack! How's Venice?" It was Candace's flat, midwestern voice. She sounded like a cold afternoon in the Loop, traffic barreling up Lake Shore Drive, wind blowing hard from the Wisconsin plains.

"Just great, Candace," I said. "Venice is a beautiful city. The Grand Canal—"

"Afraid we don't have time for small talk," Warren interrupted. "Got a meeting in fifteen. You want to start, Candace?"

Candace paused a moment, then launched right into the attack. "Jack we're not happy with the report you sent last week. Mind you, I understand there's an adjustment period with any foreign posting. But you've been working on the lira for years. The stuff you gave us just wasn't on the ball."

"I see," I said, trying to stay calm.

"Candace is right, Jack," Warren said. "I could have written your report myself out of bits from *The New York Times* or *Newsweek* or Reuters. Nothing new. Nothing new at all."

"I get the feeling you're not talking to people, Jack," Candace said.

"Oh, I'm talking to people," I said.

"Then you're not talking to the right people," Warren said gruffly.

"We need inside information," Candace said. "Information that's going to help us make our decision. We're talking about billions here."

"Yes, I'm aware of that," I said. "But you've also got to realize Venice is a very isolated place. It's in the middle of a lagoon. The rest of Italy doesn't matter here. In fact—"

"You're not hearing us," Warren interrupted again. "We're simply not happy with your work so far. There has been some grumbling from on high—and I'm not naming any names. You've got to do something about it, turn the situation around. This is a wake-up call."

There was a moment of crackling silence. I could almost hear the sound of the oceans that separated us, the push of the great continents.

Candace cleared her voice in Chicago, Warren sighed in Washington.

"You're both being a little unclear," I said in a tight voice. "Any concrete suggestions?"

"Talk to people Jack," Candace said. "Important people."

I didn't say anything.

"Candace, I'll take this the rest of the way," Warren said.

"O.K., Good luck Jack," Candace said unconvincingly, and Chicago went off the line.

Warren waited a moment before he spoke. "What's happening to you over there?" he said. "Your trading's gone to hell. . . ."

"You told me not to worry about the trading, Warren,"
I said.

"I told you to keep your hand in. You posted a three-
million-dollar loss two weeks ago. A junior trader could
have salvaged that deal with a single phone call. You
didn't set your levels, did you?"

"It's been pretty exhausting," I said. "Jet lag . . ."

"You've been there for weeks now, Jack!" he said angrily, then he paused and went on in a quieter voice.
"You can't let your personal life affect your trading."

"What do you mean by that?" I bristled.

"I don't know what happened between you and
Cynthia," he said. "But I understand she's pretty broken
up about it. Maybe you ought to give her a call, talk it
out with her. Helps to have someone to come home to."

I almost laughed in his face. I hadn't thought about
Cynthia since I left D.C. She seemed like part of another
life.

"O.K., Warren," I managed, "thanks for the advice."

When I hung up a few minutes later, I felt like screaming. I had been sent to Venice on an ephemeral assign-
ment whose rules changed as it went along. The
inclusion of Candace Searles in the dressing-down was a
blatant political maneuver on Warren's part—news of my
ongoing failure would no doubt spread via E-mail and
water cooler conversation all over the Rooms in D.C.,
Chicago, and New York—but why? Humiliation? Was
Warren looking for an excuse to fire me? For a terrible
moment, I was in the grip of paranoia, my mind full of
conspiracies and plots. I went over every word of the
conversation for double entendres and hidden meanings
until my head hurt.

But the answer was much simpler than all that: I was
just doing a bad job. I hadn't had a good night's

sleep—and I mean a good meaty eight-hour slice of oblivion—since I'd come into the country. Without sleep, everything, profit and loss, ambition, the will to power, slides into a gray, enervating haze. Also, there was something about the torpid air here, the crumbling buildings, the languid atmosphere. What was the use of fighting when even our finest efforts would one day sink into the lagoon? This was the question Venice posed to the struggling heart.

A few hours later, exhausted, at dusk, I walked over the Sangallo bridge and down into the Piazza San Marco just to watch the sun set behind the green dome of the Salute.

16

A DEAD MIDNIGHT STRUCK at the Municipal Casino on the Grand Canal. Croupiers stood idly behind their roulette wheels, boredom in their eyes. Every now and then one of them would give his wheel a good spin, as if to make sure it was still working, and a pointless whirring sound echoed across the great room. The baccarat dealers idly shuffled cards. Waitresses in short green dresses with white aprons talked in whispers at the busing station. Two middle-aged ladies pulled at the slot machines in the far corner. Canned American music—Chuck Berry—played at low volume through the speakers over the bar. The place had the feel of a rural airport after the last flight has gone south. No one knew when there would be another one.

Caterina sat alone at the roulette table closest to the

open windows. The smell of her perfume mingled with the salty smell of the canal in the cool night air. A glass of Scotch melted ice cubes at her elbow. She wore a blue silk dress with a big pink silk flower stuck to the bodice between her breasts. A hefty pile of blue ten-thousand-lira chips spread across the green felt before her. I counted a lot of money there, maybe a million lire. When she stood she towered over me; she had to lean down to kiss my forehead. On her feet were a pair of monster 1970s platform shoes, scuffed and covered in fading pink velvet. The weird-looking soles, round and scalloped at the base, tapered up a good ten inches to a narrow stalk, so it looked like she was walking on giant daisies turned upside down.

"You told me it was too cold to go without shoes," she said. "So here, I wear shoes." She wobbled back into her seat, and when I sat beside her, laid one smooth leg across my lap. She was very drunk, her breath reeked of alcohol.

"You like these shoes?" she demanded.

"They're very . . . big," I said. "Where did you get them?"

"These are chopines," she said. "They are the shoes of Venice. I found them in my father's house, full of dust. I clean them up and wear them for you tonight. Once, all the women in Venice, they wear these shoes but bigger, much bigger." She pointed to the heel. "Thirty, forty centimeters high. They could not go into the street without two servants to help them walk."

"What was the point in that?" I said.

Caterina gave me a drunken sneer. "As with all fashion, the point is to control women. A woman cannot walk far in the chopines. She cannot walk as far as her lover's house." Then she leaned over and gave me a

sloppy openmouthed kiss. I pulled away, a little embarrassed. The croupier stared down at us, stone-faced.

"You're drunk," I said.

She pushed out her lower lip. "I am drunk, maybe,"
she said. "It is because my father, he is very upset with
me. He knows about you now. He does not like Americans."

"How does he know about me?" I said. "Did you tell
him."

Caterina leaned close. "He sees everything," she whispered. "Everything. There are no secrets from him."

I didn't like the way this sounded—was the old bastard
spying on us?—but I said: "Good. I'm glad he knows.
Maybe I can get your address now. Meet the old man.
Come over to dinner sometime."

"*Non.*" Caterina shuddered and clutched at my arm.
"You must never come to my house. Promise me."

Just then, the croupier gave the wheel a half turn to a
thin, ratcheting sound.

"*Signora, vuole continuare giocare?*" he said.

"*Oh, sì, sì.*" Caterina sat up and pushed the whole pile
of her chips onto the red.

"Hey, is that wise?" I said, alarmed. "You could lose
everything on one spin."

She smiled contemptuously. "I am winning tonight,"
she said. "I am always winning. I am impossible to lose."
She nodded at the croupier and a moment later he spun
the wheel in earnest.

"*Rien ne va plus,*" he called in Italian-accented
French, and sent the white ball whirring around the rim,
and in a moment it was bouncing randomly over the
slots. The wheel began to slow, I held my breath. Caterina followed it with her eyes.

"Twenty-three, red," she said under her breath, and

three seconds later, the ball landed squarely in the slot marked twenty-three, red. I felt the back of my head go numb.

"How did you do that?" I said.

"It's easy," she said. "Watch, and I do it again."

Without batting an eye, the croupier pushed a pile of blue ten-thousand-lira chips across the velvet, and Caterina let them ride.

"Sixteen, red," Caterina said. This time the ball teetered on the lip between sixteen, red, and thirty-three, black, and for a moment, I thought she would be wrong. Then, it teetered the other way. Sixteen, red. She did it two more times. Eighteen, red, twenty-seven, red. She would narrow her eyes like a cat and concentrate, then call the number softly a good two or three turns before the ball fell into the slot. She was amazing, I was speechless. In Vegas, she would be worth millions before the Nevada gaming people caught up with her stunt—whatever it was. By the end of three spins, she had accumulated something in the neighborhood of four million lire.

The croupier stood back and gave a half bow. "*Signora,*" he said. "*Mi scusi, ma devo cambiare la ruota.*"

Caterina pushed a small pile of ten-thousand-lira chips at him across the felt and blew him a kiss.

"*Grazie, signora.*" He tapped the table, held the chips in the air for the surveillance cameras, then slipped them into his pockets and walked off toward the bar. In a moment, two thuggish-looking men in short black coats came to break down the wheel. They lifted it up in four pieces like a pizza sliced on diagonals, and put each piece in a felt-lined box.

"Wow! I think you broke the bank," I said. My palms were clammy, my knees felt weak.

Caterina smiled and put her arms around my neck.

"They are only changing the wheels, *caro*," she said. "They, do this three times a night."

"What's your secret?" I said. "Do you have a system? Is it ESP, what?"

"It is nothing," she said, waving a hand. "The game of a child."

"Still, you've got a lot of money there." I rolled my eyes at the pile of chips on the table.

"My poor friend," she said. "You think all the time too much on money."

"Easy to say if . . ." I began, then as if to underscore her point, my market watch went off, two long, two short, in my jacket pocket. "Excuse me," I said abruptly. I detached her arms from around my neck and reached into my pocket. But before I could press the readout button, she reached around, snatched it from my hand and with a quick half turn flung it out the window. She had a good arm. For a moment, I sat there dumbfounded as the market watch sailed into the darkness.

I pushed her aside roughly and ran over to the window. I heard the distant splash from below and thought I could make out a tiny green glow sinking into the depths of the black water. Whatever the message—massacres in Burundi, steel mergers in Poland, dollar falling, deutsche mark rising, sterling holding steady—I would never know.

I turned to her angrily. "You threw my market watch into the Grand Canal!" I shouted. "You bitch! That thing is very important for my business. Very important! It'll take weeks to get another one sent from home! And my boss will find out and think I'm an idiot. Jesus fucking Christ, that was a stupid move!"

She rose unsteadily on her ten-inch chopines. When

she was fully erect, she towered above me, black eyes flashing.

"You may call me whatever you wish," she said in a cold voice, "I do not care. But in my presence, you may not swear against the name of the Savior for any reason. I will tell you something—the hours of your life, they are slipping away, they are wasted in the chase after money and more money. Take all of it." She made a contemptuous gesture toward the chips piled on the table. "Buy yourself another stupid machine!" She turned and tottered off toward the stairs to the water gate.

Full of black thoughts, I watched her go. The moment she had disappeared from view down the stairs, I felt bad, but it was too late to stop her. I sat down at the table, wiped the sweat off my upper lip, and began to stack the chips into neat piles. Money was money. Money had no conscience and belonged only to the man with sense enough to keep it. Anyone who thought they could live without money was a fool.

17

I AWOKE FROM A NIGHTMARE to the stink of the garbage scow below my window. My hands were balled into fists and clutched around wads of sheet, my pillow soaked and cold with sweat.

In the nightmare, fading quickly, I had been sitting on black cushions in a long black gondola in the middle of a desolate lagoon, dressed in my business suit, but wearing the old black-feathered shako of St. Albert's Academy on my head. The gondolier was nowhere in sight. The shadowy barque seemed to steer itself around tangled clumps of marsh grass and islands dotted with empty graves. Strange birds cawed in the distance, their lamentations echoing across the vault of gray sky. I drifted slowly through a vacant expanse toward an object bobbing in the water. Not a breeze ruffled the surface, not a blade of marsh grass stirred in the wind.

At last, the object floated alongside and I saw it was the big square biscuit tin in which I had sunk Elizabeth's corpse. The tin was rocking slowly back and forth; pitiful cries came from within. Against my will, I reached down and took it dripping from the water; against my will, I unwound the speaker wire and pried open the rusting lid and took the wet, rotting horror inside into my arms. . . .

I couldn't get back to sleep after that. I wrapped myself in a blanket and sat in the high-backed chair in the living room and watched boat traffic pick up in the Grand Canal. At eight-thirty, I called Vida at the Comparini Bank and told her I wasn't feeling well, that I wouldn't be coming to work today. Then I took a bath in the marble tub big enough for an army, and ate and dressed and folded Caterina's four million lire into the pocket of my jeans and took the vaporetto 17 out to Murano from the Fondamenta Nuove.

I wandered around all afternoon on that island, from glass gallery to antique shop, until I found what I was looking for: an eighteenth-century necklace of ruby-colored crystal beads, interspersed with little blue and yellow glass flowers of the most exquisite workmanship. I found the necklace in the sort of place where they give you a good going-over through the surveillance camera before they buzz you upstairs. The owner, an owl-eyed little man with a great deal of nose hair, was asking six million lire. I tried to bargain him down, but he was being tough about it.

"*Bellissima,*" he kept saying. "Very old, *diciottesimo secolo.* Is worth more than six million—eight million, ten." He kept pointing out that although the necklace had been restrung, the clasp was original.

In the end, I gave up. Italians are not as easy to bargain with as they once were. Six million seemed extravagant, and it meant two million of my own money, but as I walked out into the sun, antique necklace wrapped in brown paper in a little green velvet box tucked under my arm, I felt a sense of satisfaction, as if for a change I had done something right. Maybe, when I saw her again and gave it to her, Caterina would trust me with a few small details of her life—what she had been like as a girl, what she did with herself when she wasn't feeding the cats, her address, her telephone number, why she stayed under the thumb of her father, who seemed, from her description, such a jealous, vengeful man.

I waited for the vaporetto on the landing for twenty minutes. Across the channel, the forlorn cypresses of San Michele swayed gently in an unfelt breeze, like half-moored souls trying to escape the dismal confines of that place. Autumn sunlight laid its white hand on the islands of the lagoon.

18

RINIO SUGGESTED A POPULAR DISCO called the Littorale on La Giudecca, not far from the apartment he shared with his wife, mother-in-law, and two sisters.

From the San Zaccaria landing, I took the vaporetto 5, packed with a Friday-night crowd of young Italian men dressed in well-tailored sport jackets and tight-fitting jeans. They laughed and jostled each other amidships, calling back and forth in loud voices, their hair shining in the dim light. Halfway across the Giudecca channel, one of them offered the mustachioed ACTV conductor a hit off a pint bottle of Hungarian vodka; he passed it to the bus captain at the wheel, who guzzled the rest and passed back an empty bottle. A few minutes later, we arrived with an uncharacteristic thud against the pilings at Redentore. The young men jeered and made a few lewd gestures at the captain, then jumped to the landing and headed down the Fondamenta San Giacomo singing a soccer anthem of the team Juventus, who had won a victory that afternoon over AC Milan.

The Littorale occupied a sixteenth-century building that had once been the chapel of a Benedictine monastery, long since knocked down. I found Rinio at the bar where the altar had been, drinking one of his favorites, an Americano—half English gin, half Cinzano, dash of bitters, on the rocks with a twist. A glass disco ball flashed colored lights above the dance floor in the nave. It was early yet. Only two couples danced to the retro beat of an old song by Sly and the Family Stone.

"Right now it is very dull here," Rinio said. "Let us go outside."

I followed him though a side chapel into a courtyard that held the empty sepulchres of monks, now converted into glass-topped tables. Reclining inside each table were wax dummies done up in brown monk robes. We sat on barrels sawed in half and a waitress, in a cardinal's habit with the skirts cut several inches above the knee, came out to take our drink order. Far above, the stars glittered in the dark firmament. We drank two grappas each as slim Italian women came out into the night air and filled up the tables. The courtyard was soon redolent with the soft murmur of feminine voices. After another grappa, I told Rinio about Caterina's performance at the Municipal Casino.

"I can't see how she did it," I said. "She called the ball in the air four times in a row. It's magic, Rinio. Witchcraft. I don't know what to think."

Rinio laughed. "One does not need witchcraft at the Municipal Casino, Giacomo," he said. "It is not an honest place. There was a political scandal a few years ago that the mayor's nephew always won at baccarat. Millions and millions of lire. This boy, you understand, was not the brilliant gambler. Actually, everybody knows he is stupid in the head. They investigate and find nothing, but someday, I tell you, they will find the mayor has a nice fat bank account in Switzerland. This is the way things are in politics in Italy!"

I felt an odd sense of relief. "You mean it's just old-fashioned graft?"

"Perhaps her famous father is in the government." Rinio shrugged, then he stood up. "It is now time to go inside for the dancing."

"Where's your wife tonight?" I said, grinning up at him. It had become something of a joke between us.

"My wife, she is pregnant," he said. "She does not dance."

I didn't dance either, but tonight I threw caution to the wind and joined him on the dance floor. House music throbbed in an unending beat from giant speakers hanging in the apse. For some reason, women greatly outnumbered the men here tonight. Rinio and I danced a sweaty couple of hours in the crowd of women, with brief interruptions for more drinks. Empty physicality can be a good tonic from time to time. Sweat and booze and dancing can clear the cobwebs out of your mind.

At three a.m., I found myself in the company of a twenty-year-old, tawny-skinned student of architecture. Her name was Brenta Saluzzo, she was from Urbino, an ancient hilltop town in the Marches. We stood in the crowd on the street outside, drinking last beers. In her innocent enthusiasm, she reminded me a little of Cynthia. Architecture should be intimate, she said, built on a human scale.

"The International Style, the skyscraper, Bauhaus, Le Corbusier, these I detest," she said, with vehemence. "Go to Urbino. Urbino is beautiful. The ideal city, they called it in the Cinquecento. And still it is a city built for people, not for automobiles. A city should not be so big that you cannot walk across it in one hour."

I readily agreed.

A moment later two friends came to pull her away.

"We will talk some more, yes?" she said. She kissed me on the cheek and wrote her phone number quickly on a book of matches and slipped it into my pocket.

I found Rinio slouched in the shadows of a doorway across the street, sharing hungry openmouthed kisses with a young black woman from Senegal. Waiting for him to wrap up, I took the book of matches out of my pocket and looked at the number and thought of Brenta Saluzzo's fresh young student's face that hid no secrets. I smiled to myself, and for a moment it seemed I might make that call tomorrow, or the next day. We could go on a picnic, motor out into the lagoon, maybe lunch at Cipriani's. Then, suddenly, I let the matches flutter into a puddle of spilt beer in the gutter. It was no use. Caterina cultivated secrecy like a rare and intoxicating poppy.

Her secrecy was addictive, like melancholy, like love it-self. Who was she, really? A bored housewife from Mes-tre, a secretary at an insurance firm, perhaps even an innocent student of architecture? Curiously, not knowing anything real about her made her impossible to forget. She had already ruined me for anyone else.

A few minutes later, Rinio and I wobbled arm in arm over to his apartment. He lit a light in the small kitchen and fixed me a Brioschi in a wineglass. His pregnant wife and mother-in-law and two sisters slept in tiny cell-like rooms somewhere down the hall.

"It helps with the hangover in the morning," he said, handing me the Brioschi. "You must drink while it's fizz-ing."

I passed out on the couch a few minutes later, still wearing my shoes and sport jacket. It began to rain heav-ily sometime before dawn. I heard the sound of the rain in my dreams, and I wondered where the cats went in the rain, and I felt a pair of slowly blinking yellow eyes, as big as Venice itself, watching me steadily through the down-pour.

19

THE FOLLOWING WEEK, a weird and unsea-sonable front of winter storms blew out of the Russian steppes by way of Poland and Dalmatia, gathered force over the Gulf of Trieste, and swept down across the Veneto. Three inches of snow fell on Padua and Vicenza; the Adige froze at Verona. In Venice itself, a cold, driv-ing rain turned to ice, sending frozen drops the size of human teeth into the black water of the Grand Canal. For days, the city was filled with a breathtaking chill.

Room service at the Palazzo Bragadino supplied me with extra blankets, a cord of firewood for the drafty fire-place, and three ancient steel-coil space heaters that vi-brated like jackhammers against the marble floor. I built a fire, set the space heaters to growling, wore two pairs of socks and a pair of jeans to bed. Nothing seemed to help. The damp Venetian cold permeated everything, lived in the heart of the old stone. Power failed in the hotel on three consecutive nights because of the extreme weather, and I awoke to water frozen in the glass on the telephone table beside my bed.

I did not hear anything from Caterina. Perhaps our tenuous thread was now broken. I supposed I would not see her again and was alternately despondent and re-lieved by the thought. After all, it was not really possible to form a lasting attachment to a woman with so many secrets. Her life was utterly veiled from me. I knew noth-ing about her, not a single solid fact. But I unwrapped the black velvet box that contained the necklace and left it open on my desk. In the gray shadows at dawn, the red crystal beads cut in many facets, the blue and yellow flowers of glass, glittered with their own faint mysterious light and reminded me of her.

Another week passed. Temperatures rose till it became what they call in Nebraska good football weather, which is to say clear and cold with high attenuated clouds, but not so cold the nose froze off your face. One morning as I crossed the lobby of the hotel on my way to work, the desk clerk approached and handed me a piece of heavy white paper folded in thirds, and sealed with a curious medallion of red wax that showed the head of a bull and two stars on a Crusader's shield.

"A lady, she left this for you, signore," the desk clerk said, "very late last night." I tipped him more than necessary and shoved the letter into the pocket of my topcoat. I didn't have to break the seal to know who it was from.

At midnight, the Campo Santi Apostoli was dark as the grave. The electric lights hung broken from their wires overhead. A battered gondola rocked at its icy mooring in the nearby canal. The greening bronze statue of a man in a heavy bronze coat brooded over the square from a high pediment of dirty stone. His bronze coat was wrapped around him in dramatic bronze folds, a bunch of bronze papers clutched under his arm. I could barely make out the shape of Caterina's domino in the gloom. My breath steamed in the air like the word bubble of a character in a comic book.

"You got my note," she said. "I was not sure you would come."

"I'm here," I said.

"I would like . . ." She hesitated. "I would like to apologize for throwing your little machine—"

"Don't worry about it," I interrupted. "You were right, anyway. I do think too much about money. But, hell, I'm a money trader. I can't help it. That's my excuse."

"Ah." She took a few steps toward me. Tonight she wore heavy black lipstick and blush, and her hair was done up in an odd sort of braid that sat atop her head like a little hat. She laid one white hand against my chest for a moment, then took it away. "I don't have very much time, right now," she said. "I only wanted to tell you I was sorry, and that I would like to see you again."

"You're seeing me now," I said. "But it's kind of cold out here, why don't we go back to the hotel."

She shook her head. "I must leave you in a moment. I must go out with some friends of my father's."

"Caterina, when can I come to your house, meet the man?"

She looked away. "My father says I should not see you again. Yes, he is right, I should not see you again. But I am weak, and this existence is so dull."

"You are a grown woman, Caterina," I said. "An adult. You should forget about what your father wants and doesn't want. Why don't you move out of the house? I can put you up at the hotel—in your own room if you think it would be too weird staying with me. What do you say?"

"My poor friend," she said gently. "This suggestion is impossible. Utterly."

"Why?"

She wouldn't answer and we stood facing each other in the darkness. An impasse.

"I've got something for you," I said at last. "Something special. Let's go somewhere out of this cold, just for a minute or two."

"I cannot," she said. "You must give it to me now."

I sighed, reached into my pocket, took the necklace out of its black velvet box and put it in her hand.

"It's what I bought with your winnings last month," I said. "Plus a little bit of my own cash."

She held the necklace to the faint light of the moon. "Yes," she murmured. *"Bellissima."*

"It's an antique," I said. "The man in the store said eighteenth century. It's probably over two hundred years old."

"Is that so old?" Caterina said, then she laughed and turned her back to me. "Please fasten it around my neck."

I did as she asked and we stood there leaning into each other for a moment, and I put my hands on her breasts under the domino.

"Of course no present is ever entirely free," I whispered. "I want something in return for this necklace."

I could feel her smile into the darkness. "And you shall have it," she said. "I will come to your hotel at midnight in two days time, and we will make love as before."

"There's that, but there's another thing. I want to know something about you. Something real."

She stiffened, then she reached up and took my right hand from her breast and led me over to the base of the statue.

"Here, let your touch follow mine."

I relaxed and she took my fingers in a firm grasp and ran them across letters incised on the pediment.

"Suppose you are a blind man," she said. "Can you read this?" She ran my fingers up and down the groove of the letters. I felt a P, then an A, followed by O . . . L . . . O, then a break and S . . . A . . . R . . . P . . . I.

"Can you read that?"

"It's a name," I said. "Paolo Sarpi. I guess it's the guy up there." I pointed to the bronze figure looming over us.

She let go of my hand. "Sarpi is the patron saint of the Barnabotti. For the rest of Venice, there is St. Marco. For us, Sarpi. Have I spoken of him before?"

"I think so, maybe."

"Sarpi wrote many books about Venice. But in one of them he says that every father of a Venetian family, when he teaches his children about God, he must also teach them the use of secrecy."

"What's that supposed to mean?" I said.

She leaned up and I felt the cold pressure of her mouth on mine. Then she darted off into the shadows and was gone.

I stood there beneath Sarpi's statue, hands in the pockets of my coat, feeling stupid. Secrecy. What sort of game was she playing? I considered for a moment trying to follow her, but she knew these dark streets like a cat; in five minutes, I would be completely lost. Instead, I continued down the Strada Nuova and came to the Mocenigo—a cheap little wine bar that Rinio had showed me, with a one o'clock last call. Tonight, it was full of the captains and crews of the garbage scows taking a glass before their three a.m. shift.

I liked the rough atmosphere of the place, the men in their thick cable-knit sweaters, the smell of cigarettes. I stood at the counter until closing, drinking glasses of chalky white wine and eating the free pickled onions and anchovies like a local. Just what I needed right now, I thought, life as real and down-to-earth as a garbage scow. But gradually a series of images began to flow across my mind: It was one of the effects of persistent insomnia— the lack of dreaming brings on a mild synesthesia, makes you see pictures every time you slow down or close your eyes, often in conjunction with a certain taste or smell.

Now, to the dry yellow tang of the wine, the pictures came thick and fast. I saw the wax heads of marionettes bobbing up and down as they danced on strings in some shadowy play; rows of ancient leather volumes crumbling to dust on a shelf in a forgotten library; fields of poppies closing at twilight; human bones rotting in green eel-infested piles in the murk at the bottom of the sea.

20

THE WEATHER COOLED. The days seemed to slow to a standstill. The lira rose against the dollar and fell against sterling. The yen dropped a few clicks against other world currencies when it was revealed that the Japanese had agreed under pressure to open a larger portion of their market to U.S. manufactured goods. Cold rain fell every day, always heavy in the morning and at dusk. It was the time of the Acqua Alta, the high tides that flood the city every winter. Low-lying campos of the city flooded, narrow walkways of planks and cinder blocks appeared in the Piazza San Marco and elsewhere, thick-soled rubber waders and yellow rainslickers became the uniform of the well-dressed Venetian. Prodi's Olive Tree Party gained a few points against Berlusconi and the National Alliance in one major independent poll, lost a few points in another. Venice, cold and dismal and finally abandoned by tourists, continued to sink into the muck of the lagoon. In a few years, in a few centuries—opinions differed—but inevitably, fish would be swimming in and out the much admired gothic windows of the Ca' d'Oro.

I chose to devote the bulk of November's report to the continuing squabble over how to save the city from its watery doom: One group of engineers was in favor of building giant cement levees out beyond the Lido, then gradually pumping lagoon water into the open ocean. Another group wanted to install inflatable caissons at Porto del Lido and Porto di Malamocco; during the Acqua Alta the caissons would fill with air and rise to the surface, creating an instant sea wall. A third group, sponsored by the Disney Corporation, suggested raising the whole city through a complicated system of hydraulic jacks.

This last scheme was deemed most beneficial to the ecosystem of the lagoon by environmental scientists, and Disney had offered to provide a team of American engineers free of charge—but all true Venetians were as terrified of Disney as they had been of the Nazis in World War II. Mickey the Rat was thought to conceal sinister motives behind his seeming philanthropy. Local conspiracy theorists, Rinio included, believed the American entertainment giant wanted to turn the city into a sterile amusement park where residents would be forced to wear "period coustumes," Coca-Cola signs would light up every campo, and the Grand Canal would be full of remote-control gondolas and singing robot gondoliers, something like the Pirates of the Caribbean display at Disney World.

A paranoid vision, certainly, but based on remote possibility and a couple of disturbing facts: more than eighty-five percent of the city's year-round residents already lived off the tourist trade; meanwhile Disney was currently negotiating to buy the Danieli and the Gritti Palace, Venice's two most venerable hotels. The next steps in the plot were not hard to imagine: Disney loans Venice the necessary millions to implement the hydraulic jack plan; Venice is saved, but defaults through corrupt Italian-style management; Disney forecloses; the Infernal Rat becomes Venice's new doge.

Each plan to save the city had its supporters and detractors. Every morning the editorial page of the *Gazzettino* printed a good dozen letters for or against, the squabble wore on, and the city continued to sink.

I allowed myself to get carried away with my report, which ran to twenty-seven single-spaced pages and five pages of complicated diagrams. I marshaled all available facts, examined argument and counterargument, even hazarded an opinion or two. Somehow, I had become deeply interested in Venice's survival—perhaps because of Caterina or Rinio, or because the view of the Grand Canal out my apartment window at dusk had worked its way into my blood. As I input the commands to send those twenty-seven pages of text zapping halfway around the world through cyberspace, I felt once again the warm sense of purpose you get when you're doing what they pay you to do. *They'll love this,* I thought, *this is good stuff.*

But I received only one terse paragraph of E-mail from Warren in response:

I don't give a shit if Venice sinks up to its ass tomorrow, Jack. Neither does Capitol Guaranty. This month's report was wasted effort, just like last month's report. Next month you better pull one out of the hat. W.

I sat down in a cold fury and wrote a ten-page response to these few lines, full of angry assertions as to why Venice's fate held great significance for the Italian economy as a whole, and since Italy was the world's fifth largest economy, for the international currency market—then I read it over and put all ten pages into the shredder. For a few days afterward, I was visited by a curious lightness of mind that was like depression but not depression: it was the sensation of ambition drying up; it was the sensation of my career going down the tubes and me not caring much at all.

21

BARGES FULL OF PRODUCE chugged up the Grand Canal. I smelled leeks and oranges, the muddy odor of potatoes fresh from the rich earth of the mainland. Caterina and I lay side by side in the sheets in my bedroom, cooling after sex. She yawned and scratched one glassy armpit. I rolled over, kissed the black beetle of her nipple, rested my chin on the heel of my hand and stared down at her.

"Your family," I said. "Why don't you tell me something about them?"

She sighed. I had tried this before.

"You are too curious," she said. "We have an expression in Italian. *Tanto va la gatta al lardo che ci lascia lo zampino.*"

"We have the same expression in English," I said. "But it applies only to cats. Where does your family live? In Venice? Which quarter?"

She turned her face toward the wall. "My family, they are dead," she said to no one in particular.

"But what about your father?"

"My father, he does not die," she said. "My mother and my sisters, my brother, they are all dead."

"That's terrible!" I said, sitting up. "What happened, was it an accident?"

Caterina shifted and looked at me through narrow black eyes. *"La peste,"* she said quietly.

"What?"

"The plague. They all died in the plague. There were gondolas piled high with bodies. Some men came into the house, they wore hoods over the head. They took my

92

mother and my sisters. My brother, I think was still alive, but they took him anyway. I could do nothing."

For a chilling moment, I thought she was serious, then I saw the odd little smile playing around the corners of her mouth. "That's not funny, Caterina," I said. "Pretty morbid. You've got to answer at least one question, straight."

She sighed again and flopped over on her back.

"Do you live in Venice? At least tell me that."

Another sigh.

"It's normal to know a little bit about the woman you're sleeping with," I persisted. "Come on. You've got to tell me something."

"Very well," she said, "I will tell you one thing," but she paused a moment before continuing, as if trying to straighten out the details in her mind. "I do not stay in Venice. I stay in the lagoon."

"That's it?"

She gave me an opaque look.

"Where? Burano, Mazzorbo? Chioggia?"

For a moment, she seemed insulted, then she waved a disdainful hand. "Those places are only peasants and fish-ermen. We are Barnabotti. We do not live with peasants and fishermen. We do not fish or grow cabbage. We do not work in shops or in banks."

I ignored the insult. "Who's we?"

She hesitated. "My father and myself."

I had been waiting for this. "So what's he like, this father of yours? He can't be as bad as you want me to think."

"No, you misunderstand," Caterina said in a tight voice, and I thought I saw a shudder run across her smooth flesh. "He is not bad, no. You see he is far too good. He loves me so much. It is terrible to be loved so much."

"What do you mean?" I said, swallowing hard. "He hasn't . . ." I couldn't finish the thought.

Caterina almost laughed. "It is nothing physical, my friend," she said. "He does not touch me or try to make love. Nothing like what you are thinking. It is worse. He forgives me for everything I do."

I recalled a line from one of Philip Larkin's poems: *They fuck you up, your mum and dad. / They may not mean to, but they do. . . .* Maybe Larkin was right.

"So he's not a banker or a fisherman," I said at last. "Does he work for the government? Is he a senator?"

Catherine shook her head. "When you know what there is to know about me, that is when we will not see each other again. Not knowing, this is better. Alone, here, we can be anyone we want. Even two lovers with the world at our feet."

Something in her voice made me stop my questions. The sky showed another false dawn. Soon, she would leave me and go out into the narrow streets of Venice to feed the cats. We made love again, then I watched her put her clothes back on, her skin glowing in the tepid light of three a.m. As she fastened the domino around her shoulders, we heard the slow moan of another diesel coming around the bend from the Accademia bridge. In a moment, a putrid stench rose from the canal and invaded the bedroom through the half-open window. Caterina gasped and put her hand over her nose.

"I know that stink," she said. "It is terrible. They are carrying off the dead ones."

I wrapped a sheet around my body and went over to close the window. Caterina came up behind and put a cold hand on my bare shoulder. A rusty garbage scow was passing below, its central bay piled high with dead cats. I saw a dull terrain of decomposing carcasses, the gleam of bone, the faint glitter of dead-cat eyes staring into nothing.

"Horrible," I said.

"I cannot save them all," Caterina whispered, and a single tear glittered on her cheek.

We watched as this mangy vessel, enveloped in a cloud of black diesel smoke, churned up the canal in the direction of the Misericordia. There was not enough earth in Venice to cover even these paltry bones, Caterina said. The cats would be ferried through the darkened city to a distant, melancholy spot known only to scow captains and scavenger birds in the far reaches of the lagoon.

22

FATHER STRUFOLI'S CASSOCK WAS WORN to a sheen, his shoulders flecked with dandruff. The deep lines on his face showed sixty years of listening to the sins, petty and great, of men and women. He lifted his sherry with a trembling hand.

"A la bambina," he wheezed in a voice like dry paper. "Salute e cent'anni!"

"Salute e cent'anni!" echoed seventy-five guests, this toast followed by a moment of expectant silence. For a second or two, it didn't seem the thimble-sized glass would reach the old priest's lips. When he dipped his tongue into the amber liquid at last, everyone breathed a sigh of relief.

Father Strufoli was not well—in the beginning stages

of Parkinson's, Rinio said—but he had come out of retirement for the occasion: Rinio's daughter, Filomina Josephina Maria Donato, born in the Nursing Sisters of the Cross Hospital the twenty-third of October, at seven-seventeen p.m., had been christened this morning in the mildew and incense-scented dimness of the church of the Redentore on the Giudecca. Seven pounds, two ounces, slightly jaundiced, but in every other way a healthy baby of the ten-fingers, ten-toes variety.

I stood against the wall, to one side of the buffet table spread with heaping platters of antipasti, feeling tired and out of place. It was a traditional Italian christening party, held in the huge old-fashioned apartment that belonged to his rich aunt. The place had two salons, one hung with green silk, one with blue, a music room, a glass-walled conservatory full of overgrown potted plants, and a narrow terrace overlooking the traffic of the Fondamenta San Eufemia.

Guests swirled around me, eating and talking with their mouths full. I recognized a few faces from the bank, I nodded and smiled, no one spoke English. I watched Rinio working the crowd, shaking hands, kissing cheeks, chatting up the attractive women. He wore a sumptuously tailored navy blue suit and a pastel blue silk shirt accented by a bright yellow waistcoat and red and yellow paisley tie. The combination was nothing less than stunning. With his hair slicked back and a yellow carnation in his lapel, he looked like the movie star he pretended to be. I tried in vain to discern any sign of change in his demeanor, perhaps the blossoming of a new sense of responsibility. But he appeared only vaguely interested in the scrunch-faced infant, now swaddled in christening robes of Burano lace, sleeping fitfully on the sofa beside her mother across the room.

At last, he made his way over to the buffet table and filled his plate. The array of food was dazzling: marinated anchovies with garlic, langostinos from the lagoon on a bed of risotto, oysters on the half shell, various salamis, paper-thin slices of prosciutto, a huge salad of *carciofo* and *finocchio*, olives and goat cheese; mounds of translucent herring roe, six varieties of cheese, pickled beets, deviled eggs with shrimp *alla Veneziana*. And this was only the first course. As we munched our antipasti in the salon, they were putting the final touches on the banquet tables in the conservatory. The smell of roasting meat and bubbling sauces wafted down the hall from the kitchen at the back.

"It is very tiring, being a papa," Rinio said, wiping his brow with a yellow handkerchief.

"Quite a turnout, Rinio," I said. "Half the staff from the bank is here, including his highness Carlo Orti."

"*Sì.*" He smiled. "This is how you get ahead at the Comparini Bank. You throw a party and invite everyone, from the boss to the secretaries." Just then, from across the room, the baby began to squall. Rinio's wife unbuttoned her blouse, flopped out her breast, and put the baby to feed. Rinio looked disgusted. "Just like a peasant," he said, jabbing a thumb over his shoulder. "You think she could wait till later."

"When a baby's hungry you've got to feed it," I said.

"It is always hungry," he said. "All day sucking on my wife's teet," and he stuffed a whole artichoke heart into his mouth.

"Tell me something, Rinio." I leaned close. "Will your extracurricular activities stop now that you're a father?"

Rinio swallowed some wine and washed the lump of artichoke heart down his throat. "*Cosa vuol'dire*, estra-curriculare?"

"I mean the other women," I said. "The girlfriends. Now that your wife . . ."

Father Strufoli wandered up from out of the crowd, and I stopped talking abruptly. His eyes showed the faint milky sheen of incipient cataracts; he looked a little lost. Rinio immediately put down his plate and helped the old priest with the antipasti. Father Strufoli had been the unofficial chaplain of the Donato family since the days of Mussolini. There was a story that he had fallen in love with Rinio's grandmother many years before when he was a nervous young novitiate and she a robust girl of thirteen, all dressed in white, standing in line with other less robust girls preparing to receive the body of Christ at their first communion.

"You were asking about my women," Rinio said when Father Strufoli's plate was full. "You remember that black from Senegal? With the huge teets?"

"Yes," I said.

The priest gummed his food, not understanding a word.

Rinio patted his breast pocket. "I have her phone number right here. I might even call her tonight."

"Rinio, you're a bastard," I said.

He winked at me and went off into the crowd.

An hour later, dinner was announced in the conservatory. They had pushed the plants out of the way and set three long tables with linen tablecloths, crystal, silverware, fine English bone china.

I found myself seated between Rinio's sisters, Tullia and Vanozza. They possessed the same distinctive features as their brother—deep-set eyes, square jaw, sharp nose— a combination which in them somehow added up to an unfortunate ugliness. Tullia spoke no English, but Vanozza had once worked for the Comparini Bank in New York, and her English was nearly as good as Rinio's. The pasta course came in great steaming bowls: a basil gnocchi in a light tomato-cream sauce, served with a nice Chianti and warm slices of focaccio bread.

"Do you have a girlfriend in America?" Vanozza leaned close, a flirtatious gleam in her eye. She did not seem interested in her food, untouched on the plate.

The question startled me. My mouth was full of the gnocchi, which was delicious. She waited patiently as I chewed and swallowed.

"Not anymore," I said, at last.

"And what do you think of our Venetian women?"

"Oh," I said, "very beautiful."

"You are having a girlfriend now, in Venice?" She tried to seem disinterested, but her face twitched slightly.

I hesitated, looked into the bottom of my wineglass. "Sort of," I said.

"A pity." She pushed her lip out in a mock pout, then reached over and filled my glass from the carafe.

"Hey, Giacomo, you watch out for my sister!" Rinio called over from the next table where he sat with his wife. Several people laughed at this, but Vanozza blushed unhappily.

"My brother, he does not respect me," she said in a sad voice.

"He's just kidding," I said. "Don't take it seriously."

"No, he does not respect me. You see, once I was in love with a man, he was a baker right here in the Giudecca. I was very young. He was married, but he was not happy with his wife. We loved each other in secret, but my father found out. It was a terrible scandal. In Italy, you understand, the man does what he wants. The more

99

women he has, the bigger man he is. But if women do this . . ." She shook her head. "No one ever forgets."

I felt sorry for her. It must be difficult having a brother like Rinio. Since one confidence deserves another, I told her a little about Caterina.

"I don't know anything about her," I said. "Just her name, that she has a father who doesn't like Americans, and that her family are Barnabotti, whatever that means."

"Barnabotti?" Vanozza raised an eyebrow. "No, you have misunderstood. It cannot be so."

"Why not?"

"The Barnabotti, they are no more. A long time ago in the days of the Serenissima—you know the Serenissima?"

"Yes, yes. The old Venetian Republic."

"The Barnabotti they were very high socially, their names written in the *Libro d'Oro*. This is a book of gold where all the names—"

"Yes, I know."

"Ah?" She seemed a little disappointed. "But of course, your girlfriend, she has told you all of this."

"Not about the Barnabotti."

"*Sì, sì.*" She brightened. "They were from very ancient, very noble families, but very poor. They were made to live in the poor quarter of San Barnaba, this is why they were called the Barnabotti, and they were forbidden by law to practice any trade. They could not buy or sell, they could not fish—it was beneath their dignity—and of course banking was reserved for the Jews. They were allowed only one thing, that thing was to serve the Republic. The doge, he sent the best of them to Crete or to Corfu or to Dalmatia to administer the overseas colonies of Venice, because in those days Venice was a great empire. The men who did not go, they became beggars or

thieves just to eat; the women became common prostitutes or the mistresses of powerful men. These were proud
people, from the best families. It was very sad."

I picked up my wineglass and put it down again. A
yellow slanting light fell through the glass panes of the
conservatory onto the thick green leaves of the plants in
their heavy terra-cotta pots. I thought for a moment before I spoke:

"So the Barnabotti are basically a group of poor aristocrats?"

Vanozza shook her head. "There have been no
Barnabotti in Venice for many years. When Napoleon
came in 1796, the Serenissima is ended, and the
Barnabotti, they are ended"—she snapped her fingers—
"like so."

"But Caterina and her friends call themselves
Barnabotti," I said.

"Of course it is some sort of joke," Vanozza said.

"Yes, of course."

The empty pasta bowls were cleared away and replaced
with platters of *rollini di vitelli*—veal chops wrapped
around prosciutto and gorgonzola cheese and baked in a
marinade of olive oil, garlic, lemon juice, and white
wine. Accompanying this was a salad of escarole, wal-
nuts, and pears, and bottles of sweetish white wine from
the Veneto. Italians eat slowly, their meals are long,
drawn-out affairs, half food and wine, half air, which is to
say animated conversation about nothing and everything.
At dusk, they brought on the main course, suckling pig
stuffed with garlic cloves and figs. I had never seen such a
dish outside of the movies—the pig actually had an apple
in its mouth—I felt like a guest at a feast of the Borgias.

Vanozza got a little drunk off the third carafe of wine
and kept putting her hand on my knee. I didn't mind so

much and let her leave it there as long as she liked. When they cleared away the remains of the pig, there was espresso and desserts and cheese and fruit and *digestifs*, and, stuffed with delicious food, rosy with excellent wine, I forgot all about the Barnabotti and their peculiar history.

23

THE CROWD GATHERED ALONG the Fondamenta Nuove at ten minutes till midnight consisted mostly of stooped old people dressed in black, but I also saw a gaggle of young Brazilian nuns and a few parents with young children, and there were photographers from the *Gazzettino* and a television crew from RAI Uno setting up camera and lights.

I found a spot at the back, in a doorway with a good view of the action. The blank wall to my right was plastered with posters for the Olive Tree Party and scrawled over with obscene graffiti in five-foot-high letters—*Viva il Topo!* This translates literally as Long Live the Mouse! but refers to a certain portion of the female anatomy we in the States prefer to think of as feline.

Two carabinieres stood on the ramp barring the way across the bridge of boats to the funerary island. One of them kept checking his watch. No one could cross till the stroke of midnight announced the Feast of All Souls. I remembered the traditional injunction from years of forced Latin classes at St. Albert's: *Commemoratio omnium fidelium defunctorum.* It was the day when all Catholics are supposed to repair to the cemetery of choice and pray for the dead—their own dead, and the uncounted dead of the centuries—suffering horribly in purgatory.

The bridge of boats shifted uneasily in the black water. The tide was rising and the night resounded with the hollow slap of waves against a hundred tarry hulls, and the creaking of wooden ramps on metal as the boats rose with the tide. At the far end of the bridge, San Michele showed against the dark sky like the Emerald Kingdom, a greenish haze of light hanging above its grim battlements. The main water gate was flanked with rows of aluminum torches, their flames burning blue in the hazy dark. The faint ozone smell of methane reached us on the wind. When the *marangona* began to strike midnight, a collective sigh went up, and the crowd pushed forward. But the carabiniere with the watch would not step out of the way.

"*Non è mezzanotte ancora,*" he said, checking his watch again.

"*Ma la marangona ha suonato!*" someone called out, and there were general cries of indignation—how could the *marangona* be fast? It had kept good time for over five hundred years!

"*Seguito dal mio orologio, la marangona è sei minuti avanti!*"

The carabiniere would not be swayed and made everyone wait five more minutes before he let the first people across. I slouched in my doorway another half hour until I saw Caterina coming down the quay from the direction of the Misericordia. I stepped out into the light of the streetlamp and waved, and she hurried up to me and kissed me on both cheeks, Italian style.

"*Scusi,*" she said. "I am late. But I have been prepar-

ing something for the feast." She held up a black basket
wrapped with a black ribbon.

"What is it?"

Caterina smiled. "A cake, yes it is the bitter chocolate." Then, she took my arm and we went up the ramp,
past the carabiniere, and stepped out onto the wooden
walkway connecting the boats at anchor in a temporary
bridge. A wet breeze blew from the lagoon. I saw bits of
lettuce and other garbage littering the holds of the work
barges. Halfway across, Caterina paused, handed me the
cake, and pulled the domino from her shoulders. She
wore a low-cut dress of black velvet that showed off her
cleavage, with a train that dragged along the ground behind. The necklace I had given her glittered red and blue
and yellow at her throat, in odd contrast to her dark
lipstick and heavy black eye shadow.

"You see I am wearing your necklace," she said.

I nodded. "You look fine."

Most of the crowd had already crossed the lagoon to
the island. We were following at some distance behind a
slump-shouldered young couple, walking very slowly side
by side without touching. I couldn't tell for sure, but I
thought I heard the young woman's sobs carried on the
wind.

"Those people, they lost a child just last year," Caterina said in my ear. "They are very sad. The child, he
drowned in the bath as they argued in a restaurant. It was
one of those stupid accidents. They go together now to
put flowers on his grave, but they do not know if their
love will survive. They must pray for the soul of the
child, and for their love, but they will not pray because,
like most people, they do not believe in God."

"Are they friends of yours?"

"No."

"Then how did you know all that about their son?"

Caterina hesitated. "Like Venice, death is a very small place."

We walked in silence for a while. I watched the sad young couple ascend the greening steps from the water gate and disappear into the cemetery.

"I suppose just participating in the ritual could help them sort things out," I said. "Even if they don't believe in God. That's what rituals are for."

Caterina let go of my arm. "You do not know the truth," she said.

"O.K., what's the truth?"

"It is not just empty ritual. Tonight, we Venetians believe the dead return to their house to eat the food of the living. That is one of the reasons we come to San Michele. It is a kindness. We bring them food so they do not have to travel so far to eat."

"Wait, the dead eat?" I couldn't tell if she was serious.

"Oh yes. It is very hungry in death."

"Do they eat waffles? For some reason, I'd like to imagine the dead eating waffles."

She ignored this crack. "In my house, when I was a child, we left a fire burning in the kitchen and a warm bowl of pasta and lentils."

"So the dead came and ate your pasta and lentils? Which dead, all of them or just a few close dead relatives?"

Caterina shrugged, a rueful smile tugging at the corner of her lips. "My grandmother who had died, and my little brother, yes, I thought they would come and eat the pasta and lentils. Then, one morning, I saw the cook throw the uneaten food into the canal and I didn't believe anymore. For many years I didn't believe anything at all. But when you grow older, sometimes, you believe again. I am a Catholic, you see. And we Catholics also come to the San Michele tonight for another reason. We come to pray for all the souls in purgatory, that their sufferings may be speedily concluded, and we pray for all the damned souls in hell, that God might show them His mercy."

"Yes, I know," I said. "I got all of that in catechism class."

"You know but you do not believe."

"What about you?" I said. "Do you believe in hell? The devil, all that stuff. The pitchfork, the red cape?"

"Imagine him as you wish," Caterina said darkly. "Still, the devil is more terrible than you can imagine. Yes, I believe in hell, in suffering. Let me tell you the story of the Feast of All Souls—A Venetian pilgrim was returning from Jerusalem when his ship sank in a storm at sea. He alone escaped with his life to an uninhabited island in the Adriatic. Amid the rocks of that desolate place, there was a cave many thousands of feet deep that went all the way down to purgatory itself. The pilgrim heard the moaning of the tortured souls echoing out of this cave, night and day, and he also heard the conversation of the tormenting demons. The demons were very angry because every prayer said for the dead releases the soul of one who suffers. The demons hated the prayers for the dead like they hated God Himself.

"Eventually, a boat came to rescue the pilgrim from this terrible island. When he returned to Venice, he went to see St. Odilio, a very great and pious man of those faraway times. The pilgrim told St. Odilio that just one single prayer would release a soul from torment in purgatory, and so the saint decreed that one day a year should be set aside especially for such prayers. So that is why we Catholics go to the San Michele tonight."

I shot her a sideways glance out of the corner of my eye, to see if she was kidding. But it did not show in her expression, which was without guile. She had conveyed this bit of nonsense with the simplicity of a child. The modern world believes in nothing, our every word is tainted by irony. Were we any better off, I wondered, for our skepticism, our precious intellectual integrity?

Caterina paused to check her hair and her lipstick in the mirror of her compact when we reached the cemetery water gate. Leaving her to this small vanity, I wandered over to the platform edge and stared out at the night. Just now, the yellow lights of the city across the channel seemed the most beautiful thing in the world. The water was high, a wind from the east blew the black waves into whitecaps. There were no stars. The moon rose, half a coin of tarnished silver over the dark back of the Adriatic.

24

THE VAST CEMETERY of San Michele glowed softly in the flicker of candle flame and echoed with the sound of human voices. Everywhere I looked, I saw groups of people gathered in the wavering shadows among the tombs, with the bottles of wine and picnic suppers they had brought over from the city. San Michele was as full of light and motion tonight as a summer field back home is full of fireflies at dusk.

We skirted the terraces on a flagstone path and came around a grand crescent of tombs attached one to the other like town houses in Baltimore, and entered the cloister of an ancient church. The smell of mold and rot here was a sweetness in the air. Our footsteps gave back a hollow echo in the darkness. The church was San Michele in Isola, an airy Renaissance structure lit by a few guttering tapers, but otherwise almost entirely sunk in gloom. At the far end of the nave, about twenty people were gathered before the studded doors opened wide to the lagoon. I could see the bridge of boats out along the channel, the glow of the city through the haze. An orange flashing light and a few plastic cones just beyond the threshold marked the spot where the church's water gate had fallen into the murky water.

Caterina squeezed my arm. "There are my friends," she whispered. "A brief ceremony—you must be patient—then we shall eat."

We took our place at the edge of the group. I recognized Tisiano Naso by his distinguishing bulk, and the pale faces of the two redheads, Bianca and Angela. There were about twenty others whom I did not recognize. Tisiano began to intone a prayer in what sounded like high church Latin. My Latin was too rusty to follow what he said, but I could catch a few words—grace, purgatory, mercy, God, the dead. There was a call and response period, also in Latin, then candles were lit and the shadowy nave was suffused with a soft white glow.

"*Requiescat in Pace, Paolinus Sarpius,*" Tisiano intoned. He knelt and carefully placed his candle on the marble floor; the others did the same, and when they stepped back, I could see they had marked out a grave-sized square of marble with flickering light.

"You see, it is Sarpi," Caterina whispered. "He lies there in death, beneath the floor of the church."

Tisiano and the others stood for a silent moment, heads bowed, then they filed out past the altar through the side door into the cloister. Caterina and I followed along behind. We climbed up the terraces and traversed the cemetery until we stood before the unlit facade of the great ossuary that backs against the lagoon. The odor of bones and decay was so oppressive here, I could hardly breathe. A table covered with a black cloth and laid with black china plates was set on the gravel hemisphere before the main gate to this crumbling boneyard. Surrounding cypresses swayed against the hazy sky. The twenty-odd guests took their places at the table. There was a place for Caterina beside Tisiano, but I had not been expected. A folding chair was brought from somewhere, and room was made without a murmur.

In a moment, Chinese waiters in glossy black silk coats appeared bearing the first of the dishes, a black truffle mousse flavored with anise seeds. This was followed by black sturgeon eggs served on squares of thick black bread, black snails from the lagoon baked in a paste of blackened garlic, and octopus in its own ink served over black linguini. It was one of the strangest meals I had ever eaten. The food was entirely black, unrelieved by the slightest bit of color. The wine in the crystal glasses was thick and black as used motor oil. There was a *digestif* of Teriaca, then thin slices of Caterina's cake of bitter, black chocolate. I felt a little light-headed. We ate in silence, there was no conversation. Throughout the meal, a man with long, shiny black hair played melancholy music on a mandolin-like instrument that Caterina said was a lute.

When the dishes were cleared away, the Chinese waiters passed out Turkish cigarettes from an ebony case. Tisiano lit up and slid his bulbous eyes in my direction.

"I hear no one smokes in America anymore," he said. "That it is even against the law to do so."

"Just in public places and in the state of California," I said, taking a cigarette.

He nodded gravely and blew a thin stream of smoke at the tops of the cypresses.

Bianca the redhead leaned forward and touched my arm. "How did you find our little ceremony, Signor Squire?" she said. She smiled and I could see her gums, which looked black against her very white teeth.

"Very moving," I said.

Tisiano waved a fat hand in the air. "But how can we expect an American to understand what Sarpi means to us?" he said, and there was condescension in his voice.

"You're right," I said, "why don't you tell me about it."

He hesitated for a moment, surprised.

"Yes, Tisi," Caterina said. "Go ahead."

The fat man shrugged. "Sarpi is Sarpi."

"You'll have to do better than that," I said.

Tisiano pushed out his lower lip, considering. "Very well, I will begin with his physical appearance. He was of medium build, not short, not tall—but very delicate. He had the sharp features like a bird, a thin mustache, dark eyes. He was not often a well man and suffered from incontinence most of his life. He kept his hair very short, like the ancient Romans, and he wore always a patch, right here"—Tisiano tapped his cheekbone just below his left ear—"to cover up the terrible scar from the assassin's dagger." He paused to take a drag off his cigarette. I heard the sad cry of loons in the distance and the watery hush of the lagoon beyond the cemetery walls.

"Someone tried to assassinate your hero?" I said. "Who was it, the Mafia?"

Tisiano shook his head, and his jowls wagged a little. "No, much worse," he said. "The pope. The pope's assassins, they catch Sarpi coming out of the church of Santa

Maria Formosa following vespers. They stabbed him through the face, but he does not die. God, in his mercy, saved Sarpi for a gentler death, in his own bed in his beloved Venice, after receiving absolution. This way, his soul could go comfortably to Paradise."

I was a little confused. "Wait," I said. "When was this assassination attempt?"

"You mean the year?"

"Yes."

Tisiano thought for a moment. "The year was 1607, if you count them by the new calendar of the Gregorians."

"Sarpi, he lived from 1552 until 1623," Caterina added.

"But you all sound like you knew the man, personally," I said.

"Every true Venetian knows Sarpi in his heart," Tisiano said. "Because you see, Sarpi saved our souls from the devil. He saved the souls of everyone in Venice. In those days, there was a dispute between Venice and Rome—the details are not important—but the pope, Paul V, he put our city under an interdict, which means no priest could say mass, no babies could be baptized, no words of consolation could be said over the dead and worst of all, the sinner could not be shriven of his sins in the sacrament of confession. We were all excommunicated, the whole city of Venice! But Sarpi, he defied the pope. He was a priest, you see, of the Servite order, and he continued to perform marriages and hear confessions and baptize babies and bury the dead, even when the pope's men tried to assassinate him for doing so. Sarpi called on God's justice to say that the pope was infallible only in matters of faith. This is important, because the dispute between Venice and Rome was a political dispute. Sarpi said that princes have an authority from God and are accountable only to Him for the government of their people. Not to the pope."

"Yes, Sarpi was a priest," Bianca said eagerly, "but also he was a great scientist. He was a scholar, a mathematician. A friend of Galileo."

Caterina put a cold hand on my arm. "Sarpi did much for politics, for science," she said in my ear. "He made the first map of the moon through a telescope. But that is not why we love him. We love him because he helped us Venetians truly understand God's mercy. Sarpi taught us that God saw the good in each man's heart, the good intentions, the soul, no matter the outward actions. The people, they called Sarpi *La Sposa*, which means the young bride, because he was so gentle and so good. And when he died, his last words were for Venice. He said—"

At that moment, polite applause interrupted our conversation. The lute player had concluded his sad melody with an unexpected flourish. He bowed gracefully, his black hair shining dully in the dull light, and retired into the shadows of the garden of the dead.

The company broke up a few minutes later.

Caterina and I walked arm in arm in silence, back down through the cemetery and across the bridge of boats to the waiting city. She left me at the door to my hotel just before dawn and I trailed up the steps and into the old lift, half dazed with exhaustion, but curiously exhilarated. When I finally fell into fitful sleep, I dreamed of black food served to dead men on platters of shining black onyx garnished with gleaming bones, then I dreamed of a shrill sound like the cry of a wounded animal that turned out to be my market watch beeping urgently from the muck at the bottom of the Grand Canal.

25

RINIO AND I TOOK the seven a.m. vaporetto from the Riva degli Schiavoni to Marco Polo Airport, with plenty of time, we thought, to catch the eight-fifteen Alitalia shuttle to Milan. But there was a long line at the ticket counter and we missed the eight-fifteen by five minutes. The next flight was a nine-thirty Air France, which would have put us into the boardroom of Comparini Bank Milan, miserably late at around one-thirty P.M., but this flight was completely booked.

We got seats on the ten forty-five Alitalia shuttle, with dread in our hearts. We would be late for the biggest board meeting of the year; we would miss the opening address from Michael Hassenreumpfer, CEO of Comparini International, we would miss the first section meetings, and we would miss the lunch. We would not be in our seats when they called the roll.

As the plane lifted off the tarmac, I saw the surface of the lagoon flat as a mirror below, and the dense silhouette of the islands of the Rialto bisected by the sinuous S of the Grand Canal—looking from this height like two great beasts caught in each other's mighty jaws. Rinio leaned across my tray table and peered out the scratched window.

"I am not happy to see the lagoon down there," he said. "I do not like to travel away from Venice."

"I guess it's hard to leave your wife alone with a new baby," I said, but I saw the look on his face and immediately realized the stupidity of this statement.

"No, she is not alone, there is her mother and my sisters," Rinio said as he straightened back up and pushed the call button for the stewardess. "The baby does nothing all day but shit and suck on my wife's teet. And all night it screams and screams until I want to start screaming myself. Babies, these are for women to love. Later, when it gets older . . ." He finished his statement with a gesture that did not need translation.

I turned back to the window and watched Venice slip into the distance. Somewhere down there, in a darkened room, in her father's house, Caterina was trying to sleep in defiance of the light of day. I wondered if I would ever know anything more about her than I knew now, and I was visited with a sad and terrible premonition: the time was coming—not tomorrow or next week, maybe not even next month, but soon—when I would not see her again.

The lights were dim. We arrived in the middle of an audiovisual presentation on Tribex U.K., an English engineering firm based in Soweto, South Africa, which the bank had acquired last spring. The auditorium was plush, but cold, and had that new smell of latex glue and carpet cleaner. It reminded me of the uncomfortable modern lecture halls they had built at St. John's my senior year; but instead of students, the cramped folding desk seats here were full of traders and junior-level executives taking notes. In Italy there is none of this nonsense about not smoking indoors—a cloud of blue cigarette smoke hovered over the pit below.

Rinio joined his colleagues in the Comparini Venezia section. Reps from the American banks were seated right down front. I didn't want to disturb the presentation and took a seat by myself at the back of the auditorium. A toothy Englishman with carrot-colored hair was pointing with a laser pointer at a profit-and-loss chart projected on the screen just over his head, and speaking in a dull monotone. The minute I sat down, an overwhelming fatigue seeped into my limbs. One more word of this presentation, I thought, and I'll fall sound asleep for the first time in months.

Then, I sat bolt upright in my chair: On the dais below, to the right of the Englishman, the bank's top brass were seated in a row of high-backed swivel chairs. I saw Michael Hassenreumpfer, Emilio Zattare, Milt Eisenberg, and Pascal Dreyfuss—these last two recognized from the slick pages of the annual report—but there was another player down there I knew from life: Warren Sinclair sat between Dreyfuss and Eisenberg, a look of deep concentration on his face. His jaw was clenched, his brow furrowed, his chin rested on his closed fist, his elbow was cupped firmly in the palm of his hand, he wore an impeccable suit, red power tie, tassel loafers; he was, in short, the very picture of the dedicated executive, and he had come for my head.

At five-thirty, the general assembly broke up into sectional meetings in the various conference rooms. Comparini U.S.A.—which is to say Capitol Guaranty, New York Trust, First Fidelity of Atlanta, and the Tidewater Corporation—met in the green conference room on the seventeenth floor.

The plate glass windows here offered a good view of the city. It was a clear day; I saw the Piazza del Duomo with the famous cathedral at one end, the gilt pinnacles of La Scala glinting in the late afternoon sun, and in the far distance, beyond the Arco della Pace to the west, the distant silhouette of the Maritime Alps. But I could not spare more than a thought for this lovely prospect. Warren was a man who expected results and he loved to put people on the spot, without warning. It was part of his sports thing: you had to be ready for a call off the bench at any moment, ready to give your all for the team in a clutch play.

I took a seat, once again at the back. Out of sight, out of mind, I thought. The conference room filled up with bright, ruddy American faces; American English assaulted my ear. It sounded hard and strange after months of the nuanced, seductive slur of the Venetian dialect. I recognized a few traders from home, but I didn't feel like saying a word to any of them. I waved, shrugged, and smiled at their "How'zit going?" and "Hey Jack!" After a minute, Warren walked in with Ted Bulley, a Yale-educated go-getter type I knew from the Room. Bulley was young, athletic, confident, blond, an excellent trader and easy to despise. Coming past my chair, Warren put out his muscular hand and squeezed my shoulder. I could feel his strong grip through the padding of my suit.

"Glad to see you could make it, Jack," he said, smiling, but the look in his eyes was black.

"Hey guy!" Bulley said, and made a pistol with his thumb and forefinger.

The meeting began with a report from Bill Snead, who had been at Banco di Roma for more than a year now. His area of expertise was Italian prime lending rates in particular, and European interest rates in general. He gave a clear account of the fluctuations of the market over the last six months, how it had been affected by the vicissitudes of election year politics.

I found my mind wandering. Snead had married an Italian woman some years ago in New York. I had seen pictures; she was tall for an Italian woman and quite attractive. He was a dumpy little guy who favored bow ties and striped shirts. For a callous moment, I tried to imagine him and his wife having sex—how many times a week they did it, who was on top, who on bottom, whether one of them tied the other to the bed, whether Snead wore her panties around the house—then I felt ashamed of myself.

Following Snead was Rick Bottoms, a new face, Capitol Guaranty's man at Credito Milano. Bottoms did an even better job than Snead; he was precise, informative, and full of humorous anecdotes. His specialty was Italian housing starts and the trajectory of construction loans in Italy. This was a tricky topic, the Italian construction scene was as infested with fraud and Mafia corruption as an old barn is infested with termites—but he did a fine job explaining the scene in a detailed and entertaining manner.

After Bottoms took his seat, Warren rose and stepped behind the podium, and I felt a sick twisting in my stomach.

"This next report is going to be a little impromptu," he said. "But I think we need we to hear a word from our man in Venice, Jack Squire. This man already knows everything Capitol Guaranty is going to need to know about the Italian political scene. Jack?"

The bastard! He hadn't said a word about me giving a presentation. He hadn't even said anything about coming to Italy! Still, I knew Warren; I should have been ready for something like this. I rose and walked slowly up the aisle, my mind working a mile a minute. The back of my neck began to sweat, my hands felt sticky as I gripped the podium. In the next second, I realized I knew nothing at all about Italian politics. I knew as much about Italian politics as I knew about Egyptology—which was squat, just what I'd read in the papers. I could hardly focus on the audience staring up at me. But I did notice the look on Ted Bulley's face, which was no look at all. Here was a man waiting for me to take a big fall.

"Before I talk about the way the lira is going to track after the elections in April," I began, "I want to talk a little about Venice. The first thing you notice about the place is that the streets are full of water . . ." I paused. No one laughed. "That's a joke, by the way, folks. In any case, the city is sinking at the rate of half a centimeter a year. This may not sound like much, and the average person might think it has no bearing on the political scene, but let me tell you, it does. The Italian government could stop Venice from sinking, but they don't. Why? In a word, politics. . . ."

I went on in this vague, general manner for a long while. After the first few minutes, I was conscious of my audience slipping away. They squirmed in their seats, stared out at the golden afternoon light over Milan's lovely skyline, coughed, rustled papers. At the end, I could hardly hear the words coming out of my own mouth. Instead, a loud crashing sound echoed in my ears, which was the sound of my career falling to bits. When I descended the podium and walked back down the aisle to my seat, not one of them would meet my eyes.

26

AFTER THE MEETING, WARREN caught up with me in the hallway outside the conference room. His face looked tight; he jabbed a thick finger in my direction.

"I need to see you, now," he said. Ted Bulley hovered

off to his right, with the air of a man officiating at a funeral.

"Sure," I said quietly.

"And if you don't mind, I'm going to have Ted sit in on this one."

I minded, but I didn't say anything. This was a familiar part of Warren's method: he always wanted to let you know there was someone in the wings waiting to take your place.

"Let's find a private spot." Warren strode down the corridor, trying the doors of the darkened offices. One of them opened and he motioned us to follow. The office was a disused cubicle with a dusty desk, a broken swivel chair in the corner, and several ancient computers lying in pieces across the tan carpet. Warren rested his rump on the desk, Bulley went to stand before the window, stiff-lipped, arms crossed. I sat down in the chair without thinking and stared up at them, sweating, like a suspect at a police grilling.

"Wait a minute," I said, trying to smile. "Aren't you guys supposed to read me my rights?"

Warren ignored this. "Jack, that presentation was a goddamned joke, an embarrassment. You make the whole team look bad with something like that."

"Maybe if you had given me a little warning, Warren," I heard myself say.

Warren jabbed his finger at me again. "You know that every member of my team has got to be able to think on his feet. By this time, you should be an expert on Italian politics! You should be able to give that report in your sleep."

If I could only sleep, I almost said, but I kept my mouth shut. Bulley stepped into the pause.

"In all fairness to Jack," he said, "a few slides, a couple of charts would have helped a hell of a lot—and those things take some advance notice. Maybe Jack's just not much of a public speaker." He grinned at me, as if to say, *I'm on your side*; but the best hatchetmen practice grins like that in front of the mirror every morning before they sharpen their hatchets. He wasn't on my side at all.

Both of them waited for me to hang myself with my next words. Bulley actually licked his lips. Pale afternoon sunlight flooded the room, the dull thrum of traffic rose up from the Via Dante below. Then, I looked into Warren's eyes and saw something that took the breath from me. I looked again, to make sure I wasn't hallucinating. There was no mistaking what I saw. I was looking into the eyes of a corpse. They were black, vacant, clouded with death. I couldn't suppress a gasp. Warren was a dying man. He appeared robust, healthy, but an illness gnawed relentlessly inside of him. He didn't have much longer to live. I couldn't say how I knew this, but there was no doubt in my mind: inside of three months, Warren would be dead.

Warren flinched. "Something wrong Jack?" he said.

I stood out of my interrogation chair, and turned to Ted Bulley. "Ted, why don't you leave me alone with Warren," I said.

Bulley seemed surprised. He turned to Warren. This wasn't the way it was supposed to go. He wanted in on this little piece of blood sport.

Warren hesitated. "Anything you have to say," he said, "it's for Ted to hear too."

"This way you have of humiliating people in front of others, it's no good Warren," I said softly. "But that's not what I want to talk about. I want to talk about you. How's your health? Are you well?"

Warren blinked up at me, then he turned to his flunky. "Ted, I'll catch up with you back at the hotel," he said.

Ted nodded, confused, and left the room.

"Now what the hell was that about?" Warren tried to sound tough, but his voice broke.

I put my hand on his arm. "You're not well, are you Warren?"

He opened his mouth to deny this assertion; no words came out. Then he bowed his head and sagged into himself, like a tire deflating. I could hardly hear his voice when he spoke. "No," he said. "I'm not well."

"What do the doctors say?"

He looked up at me and his eyes were strange, and again, I saw the death in them. "How the fuck did you know?" he said. "I haven't even told Karen yet."

I shrugged. "I don't know," I said. "It's in your eyes."

"Huh?" He didn't understand. Neither did I.

"Never mind," I said. "But I really think you should tell Karen. Maybe you should cut this visit short. Go home, tell her you love her."

He gave a dry, sickly chuckle. "But I don't love her," he said. "In any case, I've got meetings for the next four days. I'm booked solid."

"Warren," I said. "You shouldn't waste your time here, among strangers. The bank, the elections, none of that matters anymore. Not to you."

"That's just what I was going to say to you, Jack," he said. "I was going to fire your ass. Give Bulley your job, on the spot."

"Go ahead," I said.

He looked down at the floor, clasping and unclasping his hands. I waited for him to speak.

"You asked what the doctors said, the bastards," he said at last. "They said it's cancer, lymphatic cancer.

121

O.K., I'm going into chemo when I get back. But I'm not going to let this thing get me down, all right? No special vacations, nothing. It's the bastard who slows down, breaks his routine. That's the one who drops dead. Not me. I'm taking this thing in stride."

"Warren, look up."

He looked up; there was a childish innocence, a helplessness, in his face. I stepped over and put two fingers against the pulse in his neck, just above the tight starched collar of his Brooks Brothers shirt and saw the chrome-and-white hospital bed, the glittering sacs of hemoglobin dripping away uselessly, then the still, white corpse and the coffin and the flesh peeling from the skull, the creeping decay of the grave. It was too horrible. I dropped my fingers and stepped back.

"What, you some kind of doctor or something?" Warren said.

I managed a smile. "It was all that reading I did at St. John's. Harvey's *Exercitatio anatomica*. Take my advice Warren. Go home, go home now."

I didn't wait for him to answer. I turned on my heels and left the room.

27

I FOUND A LITTLE DIVE beneath the scaffolding of the Porta dei Fabbri and slumped at the bar for a couple of hours, drinking shots of grappa chased with Moretti, trying to figure things out. A fat prostitute wearing a gold lamé blouse drowsed at the other end; a midget sat at one of the dirty tables doing a crossword puzzle.

The jukebox in the corner kept playing Perez Prado's version of "Patricia." For a few minutes, I thought I was an extra in a Fellini film. I felt bad about Warren, but more than that I was worried about myself. What was happening to me? I had decided long ago, on the day my mother died, that God didn't exist. Premonitions and visions were not something I cared to entertain. Especially grim ones.

Six grappas with six beer chasers didn't seem to bring anything but a dull headache. I couldn't get rid of the creepy feeling that was like a thin sheen of sweat covering my skin. This called for a quick dose of vulgar life. I rang Rinio at the number where he was staying with a cousin. He was just about to head out on the town.

"Yes, tonight I go to a very special club," he said. "But you are warned, there will be women there who—"

"I don't care," I interrupted. "Sounds good to me."

At Club Strip-Sexy! naked girls hung in cages from the ceiling, cellular phones affixed to their garter belts. Some gyrated to the thump of 1980s-era New Wave, others masturbated with huge dildos or hairbrushes or chrome-plated kitchen implements. There was a bank of pink phones along the bar. You had but to lift the receiver and insert your credit card to talk to one of the girls. Fifty thousand lire bought five minutes of loud, dirty conversation. For two hundred thousand lire, the cages would lower, the girls spring out, perch on your lap like lustful canaries, and rub their breasts in your face. After that you were on your own.

Half a million lire, Rinio said, and you could take them upstairs to a dimly lit area of the club decorated with big egg-shaped fuzzy pillows known as *il nido d'amore* and have your way with them for fifteen whole minutes.

"But this is up to each girl," Rinio confided sotto voce. "Some of them will do nothing. Others, for the right amount, will come back to your hotel and make love with you any way you like."

"So this place is sort of a high-tech brothel," I said, peering at the ceiling in amazement.

"That is a hard word, my friend," Rinio said. "The girls are not prostitutes, they are"—he hesitated, searching for the right words—"much more beautiful. Also more expensive than a prostitute. A friend of mine"—he leaned close again—"he is *avvocato*, a respectable lawyer with a wife, three children. So, he comes here once and falls in love with one of the girls. He takes her upstairs to *il nido* every night for many months. He begs, but she will not see him outside of work. By the end of the year, pffft! He has spent millions of lire, he is completely without money, and his wife, she divorce him and take the kids."

"You better be careful, Rinio," I said, wagging my finger.

"Oh." He shrugged. "I do not pay. A cousin of mine, he is the owner."

I was quite content to drink expensive watery bourbons at the bar and watch the spectacle. But Rinio picked up the pink phone directly in front of him and ordered down two girls. In a moment, the cages lowered with the slight creak of stage machinery and the girls were in our laps.

"I love Milan!" Rinio called over his girl's shoulder. She was a strapping blonde with big, pointy breasts straight out of the 1950s. He started to say something else, then shrugged and buried his face in her cleavage. The girl in my lap was small-boned, but her breasts were larger by proportion. She had dark hair and high oriental cheekbones. She cupped her breasts and held them out to me with a coy smile, like someone offering an especially fattening box of chocolates. For a moment, I was tempted. Then I shook my head and patted the stool next to me. The girl seemed disappointed. She climbed off of my lap and accepted my offer of a drink. She ordered a rum and Coke and when it came, drank it down in one gulp.

"You have a girlfriend?" she asked in good English.

I thought for a moment. "Yes," I said. "Sort of."

"Where does she live?"

"Venezia," I said.

"Ah! She is Italian."

"Yes," I said.

"The women in Venice, they are very beautiful," the girl said.

"You're right," I said. I stood up and reached for my wallet. "I've got to be getting back there."

Outside, the night air was thick with car exhaust. The shadow of the Duomo raised itself against the yellow sky. I could not see the stars or smell the sea, or hear the hush of water in the canals, and I wanted to be in Venice very badly and see Caterina again. A moment later, Rinio followed me out to the sidewalk.

"Here we have friendly naked girls," he said. "And my cousin tells me, these two, they are easily made. And you are leaving!"

"Sorry, Rinio," I said. "I guess I wasn't in the mood after all."

"I didn't offend you by bringing you here?" he said.

"No," I said. "I've got to get back, I'm not feeling well."

"You go back to Venice?" He seemed incredulous. "Tonight?"

"If I hurry I can make the midnight shuttle," I said.

Rinio took a deep breath and sighed. "It is this woman, this Vendramin," he said. "She has you by the *coglioni*. Now it is my turn to lecture you—I say again, my friend, be wary of Venetian women, they are not good. Look at my wife!" Then he squeezed my hand and hurried back to the fleshy aviary waiting inside.

28

CATERINA UNDRESSED WITHOUT A WORD, got on her knees on the bed and made the clam for me. After a while, she turned around on all fours and took me into her mouth. An unexpected escalation; I didn't last very long. Then, she pushed herself out to the edge of the bed, sliding her rump onto a pillow.

"Kiss me here," she whispered and showed me with her fingers just where she wanted me to kiss her. This was the first time she had offered up such a request—I had tried before and been gently rebuffed—but now the marble walls of the hotel room echoed with her encouragements uttered in the soft, untranslatable dialect of pleasure. I thought of the sleek flanks of sinewy fish, of ancient buildings half sunk in green water, the sweet fetid reek of the sluice. Afterward, we lay twisted in the sheets for some time, listening to the distant thump of the dredgers clearing the silted canals around La Fenice. Dawn was approaching. Soon she would put on her clothes and vanish I knew not where.

"A strange thing happened to me in Milan," I said.

"Ah?" She nestled closer, pressing her face into my shoulder.

I told her about Warren, how I knew just from looking in his eyes, that he was going to die. "He admitted he was sick," I said. "And he hadn't told anyone, not even his wife."

Caterina made a little man out of two fingers and walked them across my chest. She didn't seem surprised. The tips of her fingers were cold as ice.

"Perhaps you have the gift of prophecy," she said. "This is a great gift, a gift from God."

"No," I said. "I don't believe in any of that."

"Not in God?" She seemed shocked.

"No," I said.

She was silent for a moment. "Do you breathe?" she said in a quiet voice.

"What do you think?" I pressed her hand flat against my chest.

"If you breathe, you believe in God."

"How's that?"

"You are exhaling the miracle of creation breathed into the sullen clay in the Garden on the sixth day."

"That's very romantic," I said.

"I do not know what this word means, romantic, the way you use it," Caterina said. "The way you use it is like saying that I am a woman who lies to herself."

"I'll tell you what," I said, "nothing like that thing with Warren ever happened to me back home. It all started since I came to Venice—not sleeping, strange dreams, weird premonitions."

"Perhaps Venice is good for your soul," Caterina said, "because it is so beautiful."

I rolled over and took her in a hard grip by the shoulders. "And here's another premonition," I said. "I think that soon, I'll never see you again. You'll just vanish back to your life, without a word. And before that happens, I want to know just one real thing about you."

Caterina turned her face away. She didn't say anything.

I sighed and let her go, and she laid her head back on the pillow.

"Let's start at the beginning," I said. "Why me? We have nothing in common."

"This is not true," she said. "You do not sleep, I do not sleep. We have the same hours. This is very important for me."

"So it's out of convenience."

"And also you like the cats," she said.

"A lot of people like cats," I said. "There's got to be more."

"Yes, there is more," she said. "I saw at once that you were guilty, that you feel yourself to be guilty. And I will tell you something you already know—this is the reason you do not sleep."

I felt an odd wrenching in my gut. She was right. Yes, I was guilty. Guilty of complacency, of expediency, of cruelty to animals, of drowning my best intentions in the phosphorous glow of the trading screen. And I thought of how Elizabeth had looked at me with her yellow eyes when the vet shot the poison into her flesh, and of all the years I had wasted making money. My mother had wanted me to be an artist. I remembered now the terrible fights at home when father decided to send me to military school.

"But if you were not guilty," Caterina said softly, "I would not like you so much. Because I also, am guilty."

"Of what?"

Caterina stared up into the darkness of the ceiling. "I

am no different from many others in Venice," she said. "I am guilty of many things."

"Try to be more specific," I said.

She hesitated, and for a moment I thought she wouldn't continue. "I am guilty of loving beautiful things more than goodness," she said at last, "of loving pleasure more than the soul. For many centuries, you see, we Venetians have thought only of ourselves, of the profit we could make from the rest of the world. We pretended to love God, we built many churches, but we did not love Him. We only loved the beautiful churches we built as a miser loves his money. We loved marble and gold and painted glass. Once, long ago, the rest of the world made war on us. Did you know that? Venice was declared an anathema, a scourge. Venetians were cut down like dogs or Jews wherever they were found."

"We were talking about you, Caterina," I said, "not about Venice."

She put a cold hand on my arm. "When I talk about Venice, I am talking about myself," she said. "The history of my people, down to the smallest crime, lives in my blood. Listen—Venice was a city of whores and pimps, did you know that? Once, there were more than twenty thousand whores in the city, from fishwives who would get on their backs for a few coppers to the most elegant courtesans who would only sleep with kings for a king's ransom. And all of them, high and low, were registered in a great book in the Palace of the Doge that was like the Libro d'Oro, only for the whores. This book ranked the beauty and skill of each girl, listed the price for an hour or a night, what they would do for how much money, their age and name, where they could be found. Visitors to the city would pay a gold ducat to look in the book to find someone who would suit their taste and their bank account. The whores at the top were often the daughters of aristocrats who no longer had money—cultured but very poor young ladies of good family who gave themselves over to the life of a whore simply because they no longer desired to have nothing and no food to eat."

"Caterina . . ." I began, but she put a hand over my mouth.

"Shh! I would like to tell you a long story, but you must not interrupt with foolish questions. Do you agree?"

"Is the story about you?"

Caterina sighed. "Already the questions."

"O.K., O.K. Go ahead, I'll shut up."

"Good. It is the story of a young girl named Celestina who is from Venice, but a long time ago. She is Barnabotti, which means she lives in a dirty little house on a dirty canal in the poor quarter of San Barnaba with her mother and her three brothers. The mother is a pious woman, but weak. She goes to mass every morning to pray for the soul of her husband who one day became very sad and drowned himself in the Rio della Misericordia, and she leaves the children alone for hours with nothing to eat and no one to look after them. Naturally, the blood of the doges of Venice runs in the veins of this family and this girl—a famous ancestor fought against the Turks at Lepanto—and once they owned many houses and estates on Terra Firma, and many ships, but all of their wealth and power is gone now, there is no money, and life is very hard.

"Soon Celestina is fifteen and not bad to look at, but she is thin as a bone and dressed in rags and ignorant, because she has never been taught to read. One night, the mother takes the girl aside to tell her about the harshness of the world. The world is such a place, my dear Celestina, she says, that there is not enough money to feed all the children in it. Celestina weeps to hear these words, because she knows what they mean. Since women of her class are forbidden to work, she must sell her body on the streets or she must get married—these are her only choices—and the last choice is very difficult because husbands for poor girls without dowries are not easy to find in Venice.

"But Celestina is much more fortunate than most. Soon she has two suitors whom it seems God has found for her to choose between. The first one is a pretty young gondolier who has just enough money to eat and to sleep out of the rain. The second is an elegantly dressed gentleman who sees her one day shopping for cabbages in the market of the Rialto and is struck with a terrible desire for her flesh. He is very rich, he is handsome, his name is written in the *Libro d'Oro,* but he has the notorious reputation as a man who has known many women and tired of all of them and long since gone to the whores for his pleasures. It is because of this, perhaps, that he has not been able to find a wife from a more respectable family.

Naturally, the young gondolier is a very different sort. He is pure of heart and passionate and very much in love with Celestina and he says that without her he will die. And so he comes beneath her window in his gondola every night for a month to sing love songs, and she listens because his voice is beautiful and the songs are beautiful, but she will not let the songs enter her heart because she is tired of poor clothing and no shoes and cabbage soup and a few miserable sardines on Sundays, because she has seen the daughters of the Jews in the Ghetto going about in brocades and silks, with pretty little fans of ivory, and high chopines on their feet, and gold bracelets on their wrists, and rings on their fingers when she has nothing but rags, and she wants all these things for herself. This poor gondolier, he is pining away from his love for her and Celestina thinks for a moment that it would be very pleasant to be loved so much and the tears on his face, they look beautiful in the moonlight, but no, she will not hear him, she has already made her decision, and so at last she sends him away and she says she does not want to see him again.

"The next morning, the rich gentleman appears like the devil in a golden barge at the water gate of her house. His name is Signor d'Anafesto. In the pockets of his coat, he has precious bottles of perfume and he has a little leather bag stuffed with black pearls from the East and he is followed by two servants carrying a chest full of velvet and silk. Celestina takes one look at all these wonderful things, she thinks this one is rich and he does not look too bad, and immediately agrees to be the man's wife. The wedding, which costs many thousands of ducats, takes place one month later in the Basilica San Marco, but at the moment the *marangona* rings out from the Campanile at the end of the ceremony, the poor gondolier, he goes out into the lagoon, ties an anchor around his neck and jumps into the deep water just like Celestina's father. It is very bad, an evil omen, a sign that she has sold herself like a whore, like a slave, to the one with enough money to buy.

"Naturally, Celestina knows nothing of this tragedy—she is only thinking how easy her life will be from now on. But later that night, she is not so sure. She is lying naked in a huge bed of gilded wood in a huge room in a huge old palazzo on the Grand Canal waiting for her new husband, waiting for the horror and comedy of married life to begin. It does not seem possible, but she is still a virgin and does not know what to expect. On the ceiling there are frescoes of naked goddesses making love to animals done in the style of the great Tiepolo; soft carpets from Arabia cover the marble floor, the bed curtains are embroidered with erotic scenes in gold.

"At last, Signor d'Anafesto comes into the room, wearing a beautiful robe of red silk. He sits carefully on the side of the bed, takes Celestina's hand, and like her mother, he too talks about the harshness of the world. He has come to make a confession, he tells her. Physically, he is no longer as young as he used to be. He admits he is also a man of perhaps too much experience with women, and this experience has had a terrible effect on his appetites. In short, he can no longer make love like other men. For him, every act of love is one that must involve at least three people.

"Celestina is not sure what to make of this. Signor d'Anafesto smiles sweetly. Do you understand? he asks. She says she does because she does not know what else to say and she does not want to appear ignorant. He reaches up and pulls a bell rope and a moment later, two white-faced whores enter the room. Their lips are painted red as a bloody wound, their hair is dyed to match their lips, they are wearing outrageous purple dresses that reveal every curve of their bodies, which can only be described as lush and plentiful. They come from the Castello, the notorious whorehouse at the end of the Rialto bridge.

"Celestina stares wide-eyed as they take off their purple dresses and everything underneath and get into bed naked on either side of her. She is frozen, she does not know what to do. Should she scream, scratch them, hit them with her fists? Is everyone's marriage night like this? At first, the whores are gentle, they try to calm her fear and they whisper sweetly into her ears and begin to kiss and caress her. So she does not resist, because she does not know how to resist, because she is curious about what will happen next, and because she is realizing, very quickly, that the world is not only as harsh as everyone says, but a very strange place indeed.

"Signor d'Anafesto watches the three of them on the bed, his face turning the color of a cooked beet, his penis slowly stiffening. At the right moment, one of the whores leans up and puts her lips on him and, after much effort, he is ready. The whores cradle Celestina in their arms as her husband mounts her. But he is too large; it hurts her small opening, she cries out in pain for him to stop, but her cries only increase the man's excitement. He turns her over roughly, pushes her face down and uses her from behind, hard, until she is so raw the sheets are covered with her blood. During the course of this terrible night, she is used like this again and again, each time rougher than the last, and she weeps and prays to Jesus Christ and to the Virgin and to all the saints to take away the pain, to forgive her for making such a terrible marriage, without love or grace in it; she calls out also for the young gondolier who cannot hear her now because he is dead, but her tears and cries are drowned in the sheets, heard by no one except the whores who are laughing at her now, they are laughing! and this makes her grow quiet and clench her fists and bear the pain. And when her husband lets out a high-pitched squeal like a pig, and falls on top of her, exhausted, it is as if her soul has been smothered and extinguished under a mountain of flesh and is no more.

"Such are the events of Celestina's wedding night. Of course, human beings can get used to even the most terrible cruelties—is it not true that prisoners in jails sometimes grow to love their jailers?—and soon, Celestina is seventeen, then eighteen, and by this time she has learned all there is to know about the terrible lusts of men and women, all there is to know about the corruptions of the flesh, and she no longer believes in Jesus Christ or the Virgin or the saints. She only believes in the devil, who she now knows is the prince of this world and the supreme ruler over men. And she has learned the whore's secret, which is simple, which is to take pleasure in every act.

"But there are compensations—Signor d'Anafesto undertakes her education with great care and patience. Outside of the bedroom, he is not a bad man. He teaches her how to read in Italian and French and Latin; he teaches her about the arts and music and literature. He teaches her how to wear the silks and brocades and high chopines and bracelets and rings that she once so desired, and how in wearing them, not look like a Jewess from the Ghetto. Soon, she is keeping the company of noblemen from all nations who come to her husband's drawing room, she learns to speak many foreign tongues and she learns to discuss art and politics and commerce as well as anyone. Sometimes, her husband brings round influential men to use her body—members of the Council of Ten, even the old doge himself—but this is only sometimes and it is a small thing.

"At last when Celestina is twenty-one or twenty-two, a son is born. He is a thin, ugly baby, the father is not certain, and he is immediately given over to a wet nurse, but this birth has an unforeseen effect on Signor d'Anafesto. Suddenly, the man loses all interest in his wife's body as a thing of pleasure and he begins to eat and eat and very quickly becomes very fat. As if by a miracle, Celestina is suddenly free from his particular kind of sexual torture. Her husband's many visits to her bedroom in the company of whores cease completely and her life becomes quite bearable. She takes lovers as suits her fancy, enjoys all the entertainments of Carnival. She drinks excellent wines, smokes delicious opiums brought from Constantinople on Venetian ships, eats the finest foods, gambles recklessly in the casinos of the Giudecca, spends the summer on her husband's beautiful estate at Asolo. She even gives money to her mother and to her brothers, sending one of them to the university at Padua to study law.

"The years pass quickly now, in luxury and pleasure. She is as happy as anyone can be who has never been in love, who does not have a heart. One year there are floods, one year there is a mild outbreak of the plague, one year Venice loses Grabusa to the Turks, one year a very cold spring is followed by a very hot summer. In July of that year, Signor d'Anafesto, now a great fat monster, retires to Asolo to escape the heat, and Celestina is left alone in the city. By now, her soul is completely empty, she has traded both guilt and joy for wealth and physical pleasure, but she is content. Then the unthinkable happens. She falls in love.

"He is a young English aristocrat in the service of the ambassador from the English king George to the doge. They meet at a masked ball, where he is dressed as the sun with a gold mask and a gold cloak, and two hours later they make love in a gondola with the curtains drawn as the gondolier sings sentimental songs that Celestina remembers from the poor gondolier who drowned himself for her sake in the lagoon. Maybe it is the effect of the songs, maybe it is this Englishman's blue eyes and the fact that he is kind, that he does not lie to her, or the way his hands feel upon her body, but there is something about him—she can't say exactly what it is—

that lifts her soul from the darkness in which it has been buried for so long and makes the world not seem harsh and strange but beautiful and sweet for the first time in her life.

"So, Celestina gives herself to her Englishman entirely, beyond all reason. She practices on him all the arts of love she has learned from the whores of the Castello. He has but to utter a single word and she will come to him from wherever she is, leave whatever she is doing; she will suffer any humiliation or hardship for his sake. And when they are alone together, he has but to touch her bare shoulder with his hand to make her shudder in ecstasy. She is happy. How long does it last, three months, four? not much longer than that—for quite suddenly, the Englishman is recalled to his country. His mother has arranged a marriage with a young heiress of his district whose family is connected with a ducal house, and he must return home.

"Poor Celestina is struck blind with grief upon hearing this news. She begs her Englishman not to leave her—she will poison her fat disgusting husband and become a Protestant so they can marry; she will sell her jewels and her clothes so they can run away together to Rome, to Constantinople, it does not matter where. But even as she makes these arguments, she knows they are ridiculous, that there is no hope. He must leave, he has no choice.

"In the end, she is taken by a sort of madness. She is completely crazy, all rational thought leaves her head. She cannot eat or sleep. She stays up all night for a week and at last thinks of a plan that will keep her precious lover by her side forever. So, she arranges one last meeting. They make love in a gondola, like the first night, then walk together through the streets of the city at three in the morning, which as you know are deserted except for the cats. She calmly leads him down an alley where four assassins with long knives are waiting in the shadows. The Englishman is not wearing his sword and moves to protect Celestina with his body, but she moves away from him and he realizes only too late that this is a trap, that the men have come for him alone. Then, she watches calmly as he is stabbed through the throat and the breast, as he falls to his hands and knees, gurgling blood upon the pavement.

"The assassins have been paid in advance for this terrible murder and run away quickly when their work is finished, but Celestina does not move. She cannot tear her eyes away from the sight of her lover in his last breath of life. He reaches out to her, his hand covered with his own blood, his eyes sinking, then he collapses. For an hour, she stands there, pressed against the wall not moving, as the sky grows light with dawn in the east. Finally, many starving cats come out of the shadows to lap at her lover's wounds, at his blood in warm puddles on the pavement, and this fresh horror wakes Celestina from her mental sleep. She kicks one of these poor creatures into the canal, where it drowns, and the others, they run back to wait in the shadows. Of course, now she is horrified over what she has done, but it is too late. Her Englishman is completely dead, he will not come back to life. She tries to pray to Jesus Christ, to the Virgin, to the saints, but she has renounced these long ago for the devil, there are no miracles waiting for her. So she leaves the body lying there and wanders off, and when she is gone the cats creep back to feed again on the fresh blood.

"Afterwards, there is nothing left. Celestina shuts herself into her bedchamber in the palazzo—she is a murderess, who will not see this written in her face? It is August now and very hot. The canals stink like rotting corpses. Life is unbearable, the sun sparkling off the water is unbearable, the warm wind in her face and the stillness of noon, they are unbearable too. Then, in the first week of September the plague hits. The plague is very bad this time, thousands die within weeks. Celestina's mother dies, her brothers, her son. Her husband dies, even though he has gone to his estates in the country. She watches all this death with a certain satisfaction. If her love is dead, if her soul is dead, it is best that the world die along with these things.

"One night, she travels through the city by gondola, looking for friends, for anyone, but they too are all dead. There are swollen bodies floating everywhere. The putrefaction of death is heavy in the air. The city has become a city of the dead that goes on forever. There is no one she loves, no one who loves her, no one to spare a word of comfort or pity. In six months she will be thirty. Her youth is already behind her, she has lived hard, her looks will go soon. She thinks of the devil, who has apparently spared her from the plague to inflict worse torments. No, she will cheat the devil and release herself into the oblivion of death.

"So, she obtains a strong poison from a Jew of the Ghetto, shuts herself in her bedchamber and swallows the poison, which is not nearly as strong as she has been told. Her final torments last for days, they are horrible, she cannot die. Finally, she takes the edge of a broken mirror and slashes her wrists and bleeds her life away."

Caterina stopped talking abruptly. For a moment, the whole city was silent. I could hear her breath, the faint, dark rhythm of blood pumping through her veins.

"That's a pretty horrible story," I said when I was sure she wasn't going to continue. "Is it true?"

Caterina nodded at the ceiling. "I was speaking of a woman in my family, an ancestor. It is many years ago, now."

"When?"

"Many years ago."

"Why did you tell me that story, Caterina? What does it have to do with you?"

"In America you do not believe in the past," she said. "But in Venice, the past is always with us. This woman's life, it reminds me of my own. Not in its extremes, of course—I have never murdered my lover, I have not renounced God for the devil—but I too have wasted my substance on idle pleasures. Drink, drugs, passing love affairs. I too have refused honest love for money and suffered for it."

"And now?"

"Now, I try to make up a little for the bad things I have done."

"How? You mean with me?"

Caterina didn't answer. I took her hands in my own and turned them over. For the first time, I saw the faint scars, like long silver scratches, against the pale flesh on the underside of her wrists.

"What about these?" I said. "Looks like another thing you share with the lady in the story."

She pulled her hands away. "I have already said enough," she said. "I have said too much."

"Caterina, it doesn't matter," I said. "You can tell me everything. I won't—" But she put her cold fingers over my mouth again.

"Please, no more," she whispered. "Just lie quietly with me here for a while before I must go."

I did as she asked. I settled back into the pillow and she huddled close and I felt her cool breath on my shoul-

140

der. I meant to ask her more—I began to frame careful questions in my mind, clever questions that she could not help but answer truthfully—then in a moment, I was asleep. I dreamed of cats and seashells and the vast sunless desert of the ocean floor, and when I awoke, to my surprise, I had slept for seven hours. It was ten o'clock and I was late for work, and there wasn't even an indentation on the pillow beside my head to show where Caterina had been.

29

THE HIGH PEAKS of the Rincons rose in the distance against the hot, white Arizona sky. I rolled down the window of the cab, took a deep breath of dry air. After four months in Venice, the atmosphere seemed thin, insubstantial. I already missed the salty, ancient reek of the canals, the wet heaviness of the Adriatic wind.

A steel barrier prevented us from passing the main portals of Painted Desert Estates. *This is a* RETIREMENT COMMUNITY, announced a large yellow and black sign attached to the front of the guard booth. *Loud music, unleashed pets not allowed. Respectful dress required at all times.* SPEED LIMIT 15 MPH. A guard in a gray uniform stepped out of the air-conditioning into the sun. I gave him my name and he spent a good five minutes checking it against a thick list of names on a clipboard. Finally, he waved us through, and the cab crept up the curving drive at a speed between five and ten miles per hour.

"I don't want to get a ticket," the driver explained. "These old folks are pretty cranky."

"That's fine," I said. "Take your time."

He was a Hopi Indian with a jowly, pockmarked face; the plastic ID card attached to the sun visor identified him as John H. Dancing Sand. Interesting name; I wondered what the H stood for. I left the window down and let the hot, dry wind hit me in the face. The yellow stucco retirement condominiums were set well back from the road. Neatly trimmed lawns showed a brilliant green; sprinklers threw rainbows of colors against the spotless white sidewalks. Glossy Cadillacs and Buicks parked nose out in the open fronted garages looked fresh from the showroom floor.

The driver dropped me at the golf course clubhouse, a large rambling Spanish-style structure built to resemble the hacienda occupied by Zorro in the old Disney TV show. The courtyard was cool and floored with glazed terra-cotta tiles and full of thick-leaved potted plants. I deposited my bags behind the unmanned front desk and went out onto the patio overlooking the golf course, where retired golfers and their ladies relaxed with cocktails in the shade of green umbrellas. A sinewy man in his eighties stepped over to me. An amber plastic visor shaded his eyes; his skinned was tanned and leathery as an old horsehide.

"You looking for something?" he said, belligerence in his voice.

"Yes, I'm looking for Colonel Squire," I said, squinting out at the gently undulating course where brightly clad golfers trailed around like bugs on a green carpet.

The old man jerked a thumb over his shoulder. "He's out on the links," he said. "Today is Tuesday. He always does the full eighteen on Tuesday. Alone."

"Where do you think he is about now?" I said, trying to keep a smile on my face. "Front nine, back nine?"

"Colonel Squire doesn't like to be disturbed when he's golfing. He told me to—"

"Thanks," I interrupted. "I'll find him," and I went around the old man and across the patio and out onto the golf course.

I recognized that familiar stiff-backed martial figure from a hundred yards away. He stepped up to the tee at the twelfth hole, ramrod straight, adjusted his cap in a sort of salute to the distant flag and swung without hesitation. His follow-through was unimpeachable. The ball sailed off into the heat with the trajectory of an accurately aimed artillery shell. He followed it with his eyes, then nodded, satisfied. I caught up with him as he shouldered his bag, about to set off at a brisk trot toward the green. No caddie or golf cart for him; the man was seventy-five and as fit now as he had been at forty.

"Hey, Merry Christmas . . . Dad!" I called over to him, suppressing the urge to address him as sir, a habit instilled in my youth.

Startled, he turned around, the prickly silhouette of an ocotillo cactus reflected in his mirror-frame shades. "I thought I'd get in a couple of rounds before dinner," he said, frowning. "They said your flight was going to be late."

"Yeah, snowstorm in Chicago. We had to sit on the runway while they de-iced the plane." I made the first move and we embraced awkwardly, then he stepped back and gave me the once-over.

"You look tired," he said. "Like you haven't been getting enough sleep. They working you too hard over there?"

"Not really," I said, then I almost told him that I

hadn't been sleeping at all, that I was a mess of nerves for no reason at all, but I stopped myself. He wouldn't appreciate that kind of weakness. "Just jet lag. Been traveling for something like twenty hours straight. You're looking pretty good though, must be all the fresh air."

He accepted this compliment as his due: he was still nicely muscled and square shouldered, dapper in his golfing khakis and powder-blue polo shirt. On his wrist the gold Rolex given to him by his men in Vietnam glinted in the sun. His thick thatch of gray hair was neatly trimmed off his neck, his neat mustache, in complete command of his upper lip, bespoke retired officer. He gave my arm a painful squeeze.

"It's good to see you," he said, but he didn't sound convincing.

"Been too long," I said. "And this time, congratulations are in order!"

He allowed himself a smile. "Nora thought it would be good to meet you. And we need to get your John Hancock on some of your mother's papers in the safety deposit box. It's those T-bonds. There's still forty-five thousand left on the interest. We were thinking of cashing them in, going on a honeymoon."

"Oh . . ." According to my mother's will, the bonds were all mine, but I had agreed years ago to split them with my father. I had put my half into the condominium in Arlington Mews. He could have the rest. It didn't matter really, I didn't need the money, and life wasn't exactly plush on his military pension.

Just then, a mechanical whirring sound came from up ahead and a golf cart crested the hillock in a cloud of cigarette smoke. It was a strange vehicle, with pink fenders and a gold-fringed surrey top, full of leathery old women whose pouffy white hair looked like it had been spun from nylon thread. One of them waved to my father and he smiled and waved back, but as they sped off, he cursed under his breath.

"Goddamned chain-smoking blue-hairs," he said. "I may be retired and over seventy but thank God, I'm not like them. Riding around in a little pink car is just as bad as hiring some Mexican kid to carry your clubs. Half the point of golf is walking and toting!"

I was going to offer to caddie for him, but instead I trailed along with nothing to do, a little behind and to the left, remembering his austerity and feeling out of place, my city shoes sinking into the spongy zoysia grass. The man's integrity was irreproachable. As far as I knew, in his whole life, he had never told a lie or not done something he had said he would do. We found the ball in a perfect lie, in a patch of low rough not twenty yards from the green. He squatted, studied the ball, raised his eyes toward the flag.

"Looks like an easy chip, Dad," I offered. "How about a nine iron?"

He scowled up at me. "I don't need advice when I'm playing golf," he said. "I've been playing golf since before you were born. Look, Nora just did the front nine with a few friends, she should be back home by now. Why don't you go on over, introduce yourself, fix a drink. I'll be along shortly."

I almost said *Yes, sir!* again, then I thought, *the bastard!* but there was never any arguing with him.

The moment my back was turned, he had forgotten me. I heard the plastic scrape as he pulled a club out of the bag, his cleats squeaking as he stepped forward and swung, then the tight snap of metal against plastic and the satisfied grunt that meant the ball had been knocked nicely onto the green. I didn't bother to look. I retraced my steps, got my bags from the clubhouse, and followed the winding brick path that made the circuit of the golf course and led to a wider brick path that wound its way between the condominiums. I didn't see anyone else walking on the path or on the streets. The only movement was of sprinklers swishing back and forth and a single dark bird circling slowly high above the desert beyond the walls.

30

LOOKING FOR ASPIRIN IN THE medicine cabinet of Nora's bathroom, I discovered a diaphragm in a glossy black case, alongside a half-crumpled tube of spermicide. Nora Ball, my new stepmother—this word sounded strange to me—was obviously still ovulating. I suppose the two of them might be able to conceive a child in the usual manner, but the precaution of a diaphragm seemed a little ridiculous. A normal pregnancy at fifty would be a miracle on par with Rachel's in the Old Testament, and not to be discouraged. I hadn't been invited to the wedding held in October in the nondenominational chapel attached to the clubhouse; I had only just learned about the event a week ago in a letter forwarded from Arlington to the Comparini Bank in Venice. I never even knew my father was seeing someone— but then we only communicated once or twice a year.

My watch read two a.m. Venice time; here, in sunny Arizona, it was only five in the afternoon. They say you're supposed to stay up until bedtime for the locals. I wouldn't have any trouble doing that. The buzz of sleeplessness was ringing loud and nasty as canned Christmas music in my ears. I found a bottle of Extra-Strength Tylenol and swallowed a couple of the pills with heavily chlorinated water from the sink. Air-conditioning from a vent in the floor blew a cold draft against the back of my legs. There were red spots at the corners of my vision. I hadn't slept more than an hour at a stretch in two days now, and when I sat on the toilet a moment later, my efforts produced only one hard nugget. Jet lag and constipation—the twin handmaidens of the traveler.

I took a shower, dressed in clean clothes, and went downstairs to the living room. The condo was small, but elegantly furnished with Southwest-style furniture and a few choice items collected by my father during his service with the United States Army on three continents. Javanese shadow puppets hung on the wall over the Navaho-print sofa, Persian rugs lay spread across the floor, Dresden knickknacks picked from the rubble of the infamous fire-bombing of 1945 were arranged on the mantel over the fireplace. Suitable digs for the Marlboro Man. It didn't seem Nora had brought any furnishings of her own to the union.

Glass doors opened onto a spacious balcony that overlooked the golf course dotted with the white irregular eyes of sandtraps. I slid the glass door to one side, stepped out onto the balcony, took a deep breath, and tried to focus on the landscape below. The architects had done a fine job arranging the condominiums in an impressive arc around the course on terrain reclaimed from the desert; there was even an artificially blue man-made lake of some twenty-two square acres a half mile off, upon which it was possible to sail all year round—and yet, overhanging everything, even the blue lake and the green grass, a pale exhalation of doom. For all its scrubbed, cheery exterior and perfect lawns, this was a place people came to die.

"Beautiful, don't you think?" I heard a woman's voice behind me and turned just as Nora joined me on the balcony.

"Yes," I said. "Quite a change from Venice, that's for sure. The contrast is a little surreal."

She smiled vaguely as if she didn't quite understand the word. She was a thin, athletic-looking woman with an upturned nose and brown hair cut in a boyish shag. She still wore her golf clothes—a green visored golf cap, bright yellow polo shirt, and pair of blue slacks with little white whales stitched all over them. Her face was almost without wrinkles, only her hands gave her away, brown and withered and spotted with age. It didn't show yet, but I could already see the arthritis creeping into the joints, curling them into gnarled claws that would not be able to grasp a golf club. It was a disturbing image of unknown provenance that I immediately pushed out of my head.

"I'm pooped," she said. "Just did nine holes. Your father is out there doing the full eighteen. He's quite a guy. More energy than a kid half his age."

"Yeah," I said. "He's always got to be doing something."

"Let me make you a drink. Jim and I usually have a drink at this time of day."

Nora went into the kitchen for a few minutes and brought out two highball glasses full of liquor, garnished with maraschino cherries and orange slices.

"Manhattans." She handed one over to me. "We usually have Scotch and soda, but what the heck, you're a guest. Thought I'd get a little fancy."

We moved into the living room and settled on the

Navaho-print sofa and sipped our drinks. I didn't know what to say to this spry little golfer. I would have even less to say to my father, later. I was beginning to regret the whole trip.

"I'm so glad to get a chance to meet you finally," Nora said brightly. "Since we missed you at the wedding."

"I wasn't invited to the wedding," I said without thinking.

"Oh, you didn't miss much," she said quickly. "It was such a small thing. A few old fogies from around here, no family to speak of." She was of that generation raised to be polite, no matter the circumstances. We stared at each other for a moment, embarrassed.

"Uh, do you have any kids?" I said. "Do I have any stepbrothers or -sisters?"

She shook her head. "Oh, no. I was too much of a career woman for that. In my day, if a woman wanted a career, she had to forget about kids."

"What did you do?" I said.

"I started out as a sports apparel buyer for Abraham and Straus in New York," she said. "By the end, I was half owner of a chain of stores in New Jersey and New York that sold sports apparel and sporting goods— Sporty's World of Sports, ever hear of us? We were bought out by Herman's in the late eighties for a nice chunk of change."

"Hey, that's great," I said. "Were you married? I mean before."

Her chipper smile faded for an instant. "My, you do ask some questions."

"Sorry, didn't mean to get too personal."

She paused and took a long drink of her Manhattan. "I was married to a man in New York for almost twenty years." She put her drink down on the marble-topped coffee table. "He was a photographer. Claimed to be an artist, though I must say, I never liked his work. Too depressing, pictures of burned-out buildings and poor people. In any case, I was the one with the job, the breadwinner. I paid all the bills, even cleaned the apartment and made dinner—this is after twelve-hour days. Finally, he got a job teaching photography at NYU, then he did what all professors do when they hit middle age."

"What's that?"

She gave a tight little smile. "He started sleeping with his students."

"Ah," I said, and buried my nose in my drink.

"But I'd have to say it was both our faults. We just wanted different things. A marriage belongs to two people, you know."

"Yes."

"You see, he wanted children, and I didn't. I got pregnant through carelessness when I was about thirty and marched out and got an abortion. Didn't even tell him. I believe very strongly in a woman's right to choose."

"What about now?" I said, thinking of the diaphragm in the medicine cabinet. "Any kids in the near future?"

"Oh my." Nora gave a dry, desiccated laugh. "I'm much too old."

She drained her drink a moment later and went upstairs to take her after-golf shower. I sat down and reached for a copy of *The Wall Street Journal* from the basket beside the couch, but something about the apartment—the carefully arranged knickknacks, the spotless kitchen, the hard light bouncing in off the balcony—made me uncomfortable. I got up, walked out the front door, and wandered the empty streets of Painted Desert Estates, no destination in mind. Inevitably, I ended up back on the brick path around the golf course and found a bench in the shade of a tamarind.

Watching the last golfers of the day, I thought for a moment of a story Caterina had told me: how the blind doge Enrico Dandolo had led the successful Venetian assault on Byzantium in 1204 at the age of eighty-eight. They had given him a sword and pointed him toward the forward mast of his trireme, and he had scampered up the rigging to be the first attacker on the enemy's battlements. Caterina knew many stories of the history of her city; this place had no stories to tell. The only history here was the few paltry decades of broken marriages and concluded careers that people brought with them from elsewhere.

Now, a foursome played the twelfth hole about a hundred yards off, their golf clubs glinting in the afternoon sun red as blind Dandolo's sword with the blood of the Byzantine. The long shadows of the cactuses inched across the closely cropped grass. A faint thumbnail moon hung in the sky over the mountains. The bloodless whirr of golf carts floated like a whisper on the wind.

31

FATHER'S BLUE BLAZER WAS TRIMMED with shiny gold buttons bearing the helmet-and-sword insignia of West Point. He had thrown the blazer over his golfing attire and changed his cleats to brushed suede bucks, worn without socks—and these were the only compromises he would make with dinner wear. Nora brought the fixings for whiskey-and-sodas and left us alone together, and we went out on the balcony where we wouldn't have to suffer the embarrassment of staring directly into each other's faces.

The lighted windows of condos across the golf course shone yellow against the cool azure evening of the desert. I smelled oleander, creosote, and the pungent odor of mesquite. For a while, two whiskey-and-sodas' worth, Father and I exchanged banalities. He asked me about Venice; beautiful city, I said. I asked him about his golf game. Improving, he said. He was working on his tendency to slice the ball to the right. They had invited a few people over for dinner, he hoped I wouldn't mind, he said. No of course not, I said. Look forward to meeting them.

We lapsed into silence for a few minutes after that.

The caterers—two slim Mexican men in red jackets—arrived with the food, Sterno, and steamer trays. Nora didn't cook. It was not one of the skills she had mastered in a career as a purveyor of sporting apparel. Now she busied herself setting up the food along the sideboard and lighting the Sternos.

"You didn't even tell me you were getting married, Dad," I said, watching her through the glass doors. Her movements were precise, efficient, there didn't seem to be a single wasted gesture.

"It was just a formality," he said. "We've been living together for some time now. Couldn't see the point in getting you out here all the way from Venice."

"Still, it would have been nice to know in advance," I persisted. "I could have sent you something, a wedding gift. Something Italian. Hell, you are my father."

Father cleared his throat loudly, it was a warning I recognized; his way of changing a subject that he found irritating.

"So how's that woman of yours?" he said. "What's her

name, Cynthia? She's a fine girl. Good catch. What are your intentions there?" He had met Cynthia on a trip east two years before, and had immediately taken to her as he took to any beautiful woman without a brain in her head.

"Cynthia and I aren't seeing each other anymore," I said.

"You're kidding?" He seemed surprised. "Was it you or her? Or do I need to ask?"

"It was me," I said quietly.

"Good God, why?"

"It just wasn't working out."

Father shook his head. "That was damned stupid of you. Should have held on to her, stuck it out. But you've never been good at doing that."

I found his remarks insulting. "I don't tell you what to do with your life," I said, raising my voice. "Don't tell me what to do with mine. Stay out of it." I instantly regretted this sharp retort, but it was too late: We were at it again, as usual, and the plain fact of our mutual dislike hung between us like bad air.

"I don't appreciate being talked to like that in my own home," he said. "You know one thing the army taught me? Respect . . ."

Father was about to launch on one of his familiar homilies—how my refusal to put myself forward for West Point, or even VMI or the Citadel, and then follow a career in the army, had ruined my character forever. But after enduring seven years of St. Albert's Academy, my only thought had been to get as far from the army as possible. When I chose St. John's—a zoo full of pansy bookworms, he had called that venerable bastion of the liberal arts—he hit the roof and would have cut me off without a penny had it been possible. Luckily, Mother had made out certain bonds in my name to pay for my college education, in anticipation of just such a conflict.

"The army?" I interrupted him now, investing the word with as much contempt as possible. "Get serious, Dad! This isn't the nineteenth century. Today, the army is for antisocial losers and morons who can't make it any-where else! In ten years as an FX trader, I've made more than you made in the army in thirty!"

He hated to hear this, but no one in America can refute the argument of money. I realized in a sudden mo-ment of clarity that beating him was the reason I'd cho-sen the FX game in the first place. If I couldn't beat him at being tough, I could beat him in the other place it would hurt the most—in his bank account.

Now, he chose a different plan of attack.

"No, you're right," he said. "You were too weak for the army. I knew that all along. Always whining, crying about something. Even when you were a baby . . ."

"Dad, babies cry. It's natural."

"And when your mother died . . ." he began, then he stopped himself.

My fist clenched so tight around my lowball glass, I could feel it ready to break in my hand. "Don't you talk to me about Mom," I said through my teeth. "That was a disgrace."

He swung toward me. "What are you insinuating?"

"You don't remember?" I said my voice rising. "You wouldn't let me come home for the funeral! You made me stay at fucking St. Albert's on account of some fuck-ing test!"

Father went red in the face. "First, we don't use that kind of language in this house!" he couldn't help himself from shouting.

At that moment, Nora stuck her head out the glass

door. "Shh!" she said. "You men keep it down, we've got guests coming!" For a few seconds after she left, we stood in rigid silence.

"I thought it would be best for you," he said in a lower voice. "I didn't think you could take seeing your mother being put in the ground. I was sure you would crumble and make a scene. I just didn't want to deal with that."

"You ever hear of closure, Dad?"

"What?"

"Closure. Putting an end to things, making peace with the tragedies of life. That sort of thing. It's what funerals are for."

"Don't you get smart with me!"

I threw up my hands, and ice from my glass went clattering onto the neighbors' patio below. A thin red strip of daylight still glowed to the west. The loneliness of the desert was so palpable, I could taste it as fine grit at the back of my tongue. The dark sky above the mountain was a theatrical backdrop upon which someone had painted stars. There were things my father and I wished to say to each other, apologies to be made on both sides, but we were both mute. It was impossible.

"You know Elizabeth is dead," I said at last.

Father cocked an ear in my direction. "Who's Elizabeth?"

"You know, the cat, Mom's cat."

He thought for a moment. "You mean that old thing was still alive?"

"Up until August. I had her put to sleep. I was going away, I couldn't take her to Venice with me, and I didn't want to put her in a kennel for six months."

He shrugged. "Just a cat. There are plenty of other cats in the world."

"No," I said quietly. "It was Mom's cat."

155

"You've got to learn to stop being so sentimental," he said. "I was a soldier. I left good friends behind on battle-fields all over the world. You've got to learn not to look back."

"You're wrong," I said. "Sometimes you should look back. Sometimes, it's the most necessary thing. If you don't look back, you can't see to go forward."

My father sighed and mixed another whiskey-and-soda from the fixings on the tray. "As usual, you're talking about nothing," he said. "Looking back, going forward? I don't know what the hell you're talking about."

"I'm talking about personal history, Dad," I said. "I'm talking about Mom. We've never really talked about her, have we? She wanted to have another kid, you didn't. Let's start with that. She wrote me a letter about it when I was at St. Albert's. She wanted a daughter, you said no—that's why she got Elizabeth. What was the problem? Why didn't you want any more kids?"

"I categorically refuse to continue this line of conver-sation," he said. "Your mother is dead. All that's done with."

"Well, I want to talk about her," I said, and there was a tone in my voice, at once defiant and whiny that made me sound like a spoiled five-year-old.

Father set his whiskey-and-soda on the fixings tray, and leaned back against the balcony railing. Even in the dark, the sandtraps below glowed an eerie white, as if they somehow still retained the light of day.

"Fine—you want the whole truth about your mother," he said, "you won't like it. The whole thing was all a mistake. We weren't suited for each other. She was soft, she came from money and never had to work for any-thing in her life. I met her at a dance at the officers' club at Belvoir. Let me give you a piece of advice—never marry anyone you meet at a dance, any kind of dance. That first impression lingers, hell it's fatal. It takes too long to imagine them any different from what they were when you saw them the first time—in a black satin ball gown, makeup and pearls. When she died, we were on the way to a divorce. I don't think you knew that."

"Yes," I said. "I knew that."

"And you want to know something else?" He swung around, angry, perhaps, at being made to remember, and jabbed his finger at me. "You were a mistake too! A soldier shouldn't get married until he's my age. A soldier should never have children. Your mother was pregnant when we got married. All you have to do is take a look at your birth certificate and add up the months. There was a woman who couldn't keep her pants on!"

I wanted to punch the old bastard in the face. I drew myself up; I was taller than him by a good two inches, and heavier, but even at seventy-five, he could probably take me. In the army they had taught him a hundred different ways to kill a man with his bare hands.

"You're right," I said when I could speak calmly. "Maybe Mom was a mistake, maybe I was a mistake, but you're not going back far enough. You're ignoring earlier mistakes. Let's count back the generations starting with you. You were the original mistake, Dad. A big fucking mistake. The world would have been a better place without you in it. Your mother should have aborted you in the womb, sir."

His face darkened. For a moment, I thought we were going to come to blows. But he didn't hit me and I didn't hit him. We were too civilized for that. He grunted and went through the glass doors into the living room to help his new wife set the table for dinner.

32

A COUPLE OF FATHER'S RETIRED golfing buddies and their retired golfing wives joined us for dinner. Arthur Stevenson was an ex–Northwest Airlines executive from Minneapolis, William Drake an ex–New York real estate man, still active in developing the pristine desert around Tucson into tracts of retirement condominiums surrounded by high walls. The wives, Kate and Nancy, were tanned, well-preserved sportswomen, both fifteen or so years younger than their husbands. Everyone at the table, excepting myself, wore some version of after-golf attire: brightly colored polo shirts, khakis, deck shoes without socks. It seemed I was the only person in all of Painted Desert Estates wearing a shirt that buttoned up the front and socks inside my penny loafers.

The bad, catered Mexican food—rubbery beef enchiladas, limp chiles rellenos, dried-out red beans and rice— tasted like Sterno from sitting too long in the steamers. Nora's margaritas, however, made the right way with fresh lime juice, Cointreau, and Cuervo 1800, and served on the rocks in salted glasses, tasted like they were supposed to taste. I drank several of these and barely touched the food on my plate. Over the salty rim of my glass, I watched Stevenson and Drake and their wives chewing the tough enchiladas with their expensive capped teeth. Conversation gave way to the sound of chewing. My father and I tried to avoid looking each other in the eyes.

"Hard to believe it's Christmas," Stevenson's wife said in between bites. "That's the only thing I miss, living out here."

"Yes, it would be nice to see a white Christmas," Drake's wife said.

" 'Just like the ones I used to know,' " sang Stevenson in a warbling baritone, " 'where . . . somethings glisten and children listen . . .' "

" '. . . to hear sleighbells in the snow,' " Nora chimed in.

"Hell, no sleigh bells here," Father said. "It's seventy-five degrees right now. Least Christmas-like place I can think of."

"Actually, all of that, the sleigh bells, the fir trees, the snow, that's pagan stuff," I said just to disagree with him. "If you want the truth, the climate in Arizona is just about the climate of the original Christmas." I was surprisingly drunk now, slurring my words a little; those margaritas were dangerous. "No, really, think of Bethlehem. Israel is a very arid country. That landscape's not too different from here."

Father scowled at me down the length of the table, and for the first time since my arrival, our eyes met for longer than a second. In that moment, I saw there was something wrong with him. Just as I had seen with Warren, but different—it was not a vision of the grave, but of red and swollen tissue, covered with a thin layer of unhealthy mucus. This brief flash set the margaritas and the Scotch I'd had earlier churning in my stomach. I put my drink down on the tablecloth, nearly gagging on bile.

"Dad," I managed. "You're sick."

He blinked at me. "I don't know what you're talking about," he said, but his lower lip trembled a little.

"Are you unwell, Jim?" Stevenson said, concern in his voice.

Suddenly, everyone stopped chewing. The specter of disease sent a faint shudder of fear around the table.

There is no topic more dreaded in a retirement community than serious illness, which was the beginning of the inevitable slide to the grave.

"Tell us, Jimmy, is something wrong?" Drake's wife said, moving away from him a little.

"No, really I'm fine," Father said impatiently. "You want to talk about sick, this is just another one of my son's sick jokes."

"Your father's health is not something we joke about," Nora said to me.

Before I could respond, Drake hit the table lightly with three fingers. "Wait a minute," he said to Father, "you drive a new Riviera, silver-gray, don't you?"

"Yes," Father said.

"I thought that was your car," Drake said. "I saw it parked in the lot out front of Dr. Singh's office the other day. That was your car, am I right?"

Father seemed confused. Nora put her hand over his. "If Jimmy went to Dr. Singh, I think that's a private matter. Don't you, Bill?" She said this to Drake, but she glowered over at me.

"If something's wrong," Stevenson's wife said, "you really ought to share it with your friends, your family. Especially if it's contagious."

Father looked down at his plate, embarrassed. "All right," he said. "I went in for a checkup. Nothing serious. Nothing at all. A couple of tests."

I was enjoying the consternation just a little. My stomach felt weird, a chill began to crawl up the back of my neck. I gulped down the rest of my margarita to keep the creepy feeling at bay.

"You'll be going back," I said, after a moment. "Nothing serious yet, but you'd better get it taken care of soon."

Father stared at me, an expression somewhere between anger and amazement on his face.

"O.K.," Nora said. "Let's talk about something else." But no one felt like talking much after that.

A little before midnight, there was a knock at the door of the guest bedroom where I was trying to sleep. I clambered out of the rock-hard sleeper sofa and opened the door. Nora stood there, hands in the pocket of her housecoat. Her face looked pinched and haggard without the carefully applied makeup she'd been wearing all day.

"I've just been talking to your father," she said. "He's very upset."

"Oh?"

"That was privileged information, about his health, I mean. We'd really appreciate it if you didn't share it with anyone else."

"What's wrong with him?" I said.

She gave me a strange look. "Don't you know, since you've been talking to his doctor."

"No, I don't know," I said.

She sighed. "Dr. Singh thinks it's a mild case of colitis. There's been some rectal bleeding. We're waiting for the results of the biopsy . . ." She hesitated. "It could be cancer."

I shook my head. "It's not cancer," I said. "Don't worry. Tell Dad he'll live, but he'll have to change his diet. No more red meat. More whole grains, vegetables. Things like that."

She was silent for an uncomfortable moment. She looked away and then back at me. I knew what was coming next.

"There's another thing," she said. "Your father and I

have been talking. And we think you should leave to-morrow morning."

"You're kicking me out three days before Christmas," I said. "Is that it?"

"We're not kicking you out," she said. "We just think it would be better for everyone if you leave as soon as possible. Your father is very upset. He's been very nervous because of these tests, and now you've upset him terribly. You don't treat him right, you don't treat him with any respect and you've been talking to his doctor behind his back for reasons of your own. You want my opinion?" She leaned close and I could smell the foul pasty odor of her gums. "I think you're a real little bastard. That's what I think!"

She stood there for a tense moment, trembling, hands out of the pockets of her housecoat now, fists clenched. I thought of a suitable retort, but didn't utter it. At last, I nodded wearily. The whole trip had been a mistake. A foolish gesture. There are certain wounds of the past that can never be healed, that are too much a part of the fabric of our souls.

"I'll start packing now," I said. "Don't worry about driving me to the airport. I'll call a cab."

A pale blue dawn showed over the links. The peaks of the Rincons were vague and colorless against the pale sky. Soon the dark would burn off and give way to an-other beautiful, clear day with temperatures in the low eighties. Modern air travel brought too many discom-fiting juxtapositions. Venice's wet wintry murk one day, Arizona's desert brightness the next. It should have taken months, this journey, not hours. How much better to cross oceans with the wind, see the landscape passing, mile by mile, the country changing until the destination is reached. More time to think, sort things out.

I closed the bathroom window, brushed my teeth, shaved. Then, on a wicked impulse, I removed Nora's diaphragm from its glossy black case in the medicine cabinet, rooted around until I found a safety pin in a box of bandages and stuck the diaphragm full of tiny holes. I took the tube of spermicide, squeezed it out in the toilet, carefully pushed the crumpled tube back open with a Q-Tip, filled it back up with shampoo, then replaced everything as it had been. *You never know*, I told my face in the mirror, *you might get that sister yet.*

I dressed, ate some Raisin Bran in the spotless kitchen and went down into the street with my suitcase to wait for the cab. I sat at the curb with the neighbor's *Tucson Citizen* and read the financial page. The yen was up against the dollar, the deutsche mark down, the French franc holding steady, and the lira up. The first sprinklers of the morning went on down the street, and I thought I heard the faint whirr of a golf cart. Somehow, just by looking into their eyes, I could tell if people were sick or dying, even if they didn't know the truth themselves. Where did it come from, this terrible gift, this strange connection to death?

My father and stepmother were still asleep in the air-conditioned dimness of the master bedroom. It was better this way. I didn't suppose I'd be seeing either of them again.

33

VENICE IN JANUARY WAS deserted, a tomb. So quiet, you could almost hear the sound of the palazzos crumbling into the black water, their pilings turning to mush after centuries embedded in the cold, salty mud of the lagoon.

At the *traghettos* along the Riva degli Schiavoni, gondolas bumped against the fading candy-striped moorings, their cockpits covered tightly with oiled canvas tarps. Half the shops in the city were shuttered and closed, as were most of the restaurants; the few of the latter remaining open only served dinner and only in the early hours of the evening. Even the Piazza San Marco was empty, given over to the pigeons who huddled, shivering and neglected, beneath the arcade in front of Florian's.

The weeks between New Year's and the beginning of Carnival in February were the loneliest time of the year. In a city that lived off tourists, the only time for the residents to become tourists themselves, was when the tourists did not come. Every Venetian who could afford the price of a train ticket had gone to the Italian Alps to ski. It was an odd fact that many native Venetians were avid skiers—merely because the height of ski season occurred during Venice's lowest ebb, when the city was a ghost town.

The corridors of the Comparini Bank echoed with my footsteps on these dull January afternoons. The offices were dark and uninhabited, the building staffed by a skeleton crew of a few clerks, a secretary, one security guard. Poor Rinio, who could not afford a ski vacation this year because of the baby, came in for two or three hours in the morning a couple of days a week, pushed some papers around his desk, made a few half-hearted phone calls. Even his love affairs were put on hold during this dreary season.

"What is the point of exerting yourself," he said to me one morning. "Venice, she sleeps." He waved out the window to the brooding skies, the mist of rain blowing across the rooftops, the sluggish gray waters empty of every kind of vessel except the occasional forlorn vaporetto, the dull green dome of the Salute that covered only a shadowy vacancy.

"Yes, Rinio," I said. "Venice may sleep, but the world financial markets don't sleep. They're up all night, every night, twenty-four hours, three-sixty-five a year."

Rino shook his head at these grim pronouncements. "This attitude is very bad," he said. "It is why you Americans are all so unhappy. You think too much of making money and not enough of more important things."

"More important than money?" I said straight-faced. "Like what?"

"Like food, like wine. Women . . ."

There was a thousand years of Italian philosophy behind his cynicism, but I had a career to save. I spent the first two weeks of January in aggressive trading, screaming at brokers over the board, trading deutsche marks against yen, lira against dollar and Belgian francs against French francs, until long after a wintry dark descended over the islands of the Rialto. For a few hours, I even managed to recapture some of the old enthusiasm.

One afternoon, I posted a half-million profit for the Comparini Bank by going long on sterling when the cable traders were selling short. I felt like cracking a bottle of champagne, but there was no one in Venice to crack one with. Rinio was busy with his family and I hadn't heard from Caterina for more than a month, since before Christmas—even though she knew I was supposed to return from the States the day after New Year's. I allowed myself a moment of panic over this, then the moment passed and the panic subsided. Surely, she was at Pieve di Cadore or Zuglio or Tolmezzo, skiing with the rest. I would hear from her soon enough.

In between trades, I worked on January's report. It was, I thought, shaping up to be the best one so far—a close analysis of the latest developments rounded off nicely with an educated hunch:

The political race between Freedom Alliance and the Olive Tree still tracked as close as ever, but cracks were beginning to show in Berlusconi's new coalition. Gianfranco Fini, the leader of the far right, was now widely seen as a contender for the philosophical leadership of the Freedom Alliance. Also, Umberto Bossi's Northern League, a key vote-getter in the industrialized regions, had launched an all-out attack on anything that stood for a strong central government, anything attached to Rome, which included Berlusconi and all his cronies. Meanwhile, the Olive Tree Party was just as divided. Hard-line Marxists of the Refoundation Party were alienating moderate voters; there were rumors of a fatal tension between Romano Prodi and a major supporter, Massimo D'Alma, leader of the Democratic Party of the Left. . . .

In short, I was just as confused as ever about the whole scene until I saw Prodi give a speech on television at a cemetery for World War I dead near Monte Grappa in the Veneto. Wind from the mountains whipped Prodi's poorly cut hair, he was round-faced and bespectacled. He wore a rather shabby blue topcoat and an awkward jacket of greenish houndstooth, his tie a garish red and yellow paisley. His manner showed all the stiffness of the lecturing academic, he had none of the ease or commanding presence of Berlusconi—but he had something Italian politics desperately needed. It was the thing that Berlusconi lacked, with his five-thousand-dollar custom-tailored suits and gleaming tycoon smile, the thing that all the money in the world could not buy: sincerity.

The polls were still even, but now my guts were pulling me to the left. *Although there has not been a left-leaning government in Italy since 1945,* I wrote in my report, *and the vagaries of the Italian political scene make a definite prediction premature at this point, I believe the mood of the country is in favor of sweeping electoral change. . . .*

I filed early, on the tenth. For five days, I heard nothing from Washington. My emotions ran the spectrum from quaking self-doubt to outright defiance. To hell with Warren if he doesn't like the report. I'll sell this one to the *International Herald Tribune* as news analysis. Then I got a phone call from Ramona Fielding, a pert, intelligent young woman, fresh out of Vassar, who was Warren's new personal assistant. The last one had left under a cloud, amid rumors of sexual harassment, an affair gone sour.

"I don't think you know what's been happening here, Jack," Ramona said when I asked her about my report. "I'm afraid no one's read anything. Actually, I have some bad news. That's why I'm calling."

I felt my stomach drop.

"It's Warren. He went into the hospital a couple of days before New Year's. They've diagnosed stage-five lymphatic cancer. Apparently, it's inoperable. Right now, he's on a steady diet of painkillers. It doesn't look too good."

I was silent for a few seconds, taking it all in. I had

known since Milan, but to have my prescience confirmed like this was a shock.

"Jack, are you O.K.?" Ramona said.

"Yes," I said.

"I understand . . ." She was a bit hesitant. "I understand he was a friend of yours?" She was young and new to the game, but she had already realized there were no real friends in business.

"Yes, he was," I said.

"He's at Sibley. I've got the address if you want to send a card. I could arrange for some flowers from here in your name if you like."

"Yes, please, do that."

"So the lira project is on hold right now, that's what I've been told to tell you. Warren was personally responsible for the whole thing, you know how he is, always hates to delegate authority. In any case, he was liaising directly with the board of Comparini International, with no intermediaries and no support. Until they can find someone to replace him, you're on your own over there. Shouldn't be too long, though, a few weeks, a month. They're asking you to sit tight. I understand they're thinking of Ted Bulley to pick up where Warren left off. That was on Warren's recommendation. One of the last things he did before he left."

I hung up the phone a few minutes later and stared out the window at the gray Venetian sky. Warren, the poor bastard. He had always been so tough and vigorous, healthy as a mule, always ready to kick somebody's ass just for the pleasure of kicking, always imposing his will on the weaker natures of his subordinates. Death would come for him hard and sharp when it came. And who would mourn him when he was gone? His business associates, his wife, the personal assistants he sometimes slept with? Maybe his wife, but not for long. She was young, she would remarry. There were no kids, there hadn't been any time.

You could fault him for many things, but not for his energy or his dedication. All the years I'd known him at the bank, he had never taken more than a week off, never used more than a day of sick leave at a time. And certainly no extraneous thoughts of death had ever slowed his forward drive. But could he be blamed for this particular blindness? Which of us ever spares a thought for death? That's what Prozac was for. Meanwhile, a dam bursts in the sunless mountains above Disneyland, a massive wall of water is bearing down with increasing speed, black water heavy with the billions of souls that have ever lived, and no one looks up, not Warren, not me; and no one sees the darkening shadow on the ground.

I left the office early and went for a couple of glasses of white wine and a bite of pickled octopus at the Mocenigo, one of the few places in the city still doing regular business because it did not cater to those patrons who could afford to spend the month of January on the slopes. Now, the bargemen and *traghetto* operators stood leaning against the counter, smoke from their cigarettes billowing in fantastic clouds beneath the pressed tin ceiling. I listened to the sound of their talk and laughter and tried to think things through, to figure out where I would stand when Bulley took over Warren's position; what the board would decide to do with me—but found myself thinking only of Caterina.

Behind the bar hung a yellowing map of Venice and the lagoon, surrounded by dusty clusters of plastic grapes. I still had no idea where she lived. In the lagoon somewhere, but not Chioggia or Burano or Mazzorbo. Where else? I strained my eyes, studying the yellow map for a clue. The lagoon was full of islands, over a thousand of them, many of them off the main vaporetto routes but inhabited. It was no use.

I paid for my wine and went back through the deserted city to my hotel. My rooms were cold and dark. I sat in the darkened salon in a high-backed chair in my coat for fifteen minutes, feeling the cold seeping through the ancient marble floors into the soles of my shoes. The clock ticked from the mantel, water dripped from the sink in the bathroom. Perhaps it was already over with Caterina. Perhaps I would never see her again and it would end like this, in uncertainty. Never knowing why, never knowing a thing about her. No! I sat forward with a start, and for a moment, the dark room seemed to be full of light, as if one of those cartoon lightbulbs had just gone off over my head. I knew how to find her. Of course, it was easy.

And when I found her at last, when I knocked at the door of her father's house in my best conservative pin-striped suit and my finest silk tie, I would bring a dozen winter roses, red to show the intensity of my passion; and in a small velvet box a ring with a big blue diamond to show the sincerity of my belief that we could be happy together. And I would ask her then and there to be my wife.

34

THE SCRUFFY, SNUB-NOSED TABBY crossed the Campo San Canciano at a purposeful trot and headed off in the direction of the Rio dei Mendicanti. I couldn't be sure, but this one probably had a mean street-cat disposition and wary yellow eyes like all the other cats in Venice. They are an especially secretive breed, hardened by city life, and do not like being followed—the trick was to stay close enough without getting too close. Too close, and the cat would dart off down the nearest drain or disappear into a grated passageway; too far and I would lose it to the shadows and darkness of three a.m.

Once the cat stopped to gnaw for fleas at its hind quarters, once to lap at a puddle. I stepped into a shadow and waited, holding my breath. It looked up, ears back, sniffing the wind, then moved off with a shrug of tail. I managed to stay downwind and undetected, just a hundred feet back, for the next ten minutes. But this cat was not being very cautious. It eschewed the safer shadows of the palazzos for the plain middle of the street; it acted like a cat on its way to a good meal and a howl with some friends, and it didn't care who knew. The cat's attitude, more than anything else, made it a good candidate: after a week of following cats in the small hours of the morning, I thought I could tell the difference between a cat going somewhere and a cat going nowhere at all.

The cat suddenly picked up its pace and darted into the warren of squat buildings just the other side of the Mendicanti. I missed it for a few seconds, then caught sight of its dingy brown coat flashing dully in the light of a lone streetlamp up ahead. The streets were dark and nameless. Being lost in Venice at night is a little like being snow-blind, the same stagnant canals and decrepit palazzos on every side.

I guessed myself to be somewhere due north of the Piazza San Marco, in the vicinity of San Zanipolo, the massive church where Venice's doges are entombed, their bones turning to dust in ornate sarcophaguses. There also, in a tiny coffin of rose marble, folded up neat as a table napkin, lies the flayed skin of the great Admiral Bragadino, after whom my hotel was named. Following the brave and desperate defense of Famagusta in Cyprus, Bragadino surrendered to the Turkish commander Lala Mustafa with the assurance that he and his men would be spared and allowed safe passage back to Venice. But his men were immediately hacked to pieces, he was tortured slowly for days then skinned alive, and his skin was tanned and stuffed with straw and sent back to Constantinople as a grisly trophy of war. Later, it was stolen back by secret agents of Venice, posing as traitors turned Turk, and laid to rest within Zanipolo's thick walls.

"You must learn from the fate of poor Bragadino a lesson," Caterina had said after relating this horrible episode. "Never, never trust a Turk."

Now, the cat stopped and pointed its flat nose at the waning moon. I thought I recognized something familiar here, something about the soot-black, crooked walls, the canal below silted up with sludge, the vague scent of putrefaction in the air. Then, I heard a low, feline murmur that was like all the cats in the world purring at once, and I knew we were there. I left my concealment in the shadows and marched forward. The cat jerked around and gave an outraged cry when it saw me coming on.

"Scat!" I said. "I know the way from here."

The cat stood its ground for a moment, ears flat, hissing, then I stamped my foot and it scurried off.

In truth, my pronouncement was a little premature. It took me another ten minutes, though I was never out of earshot of the cat sound. After a series of feints down blind alleys and one misstep over a little bridge that almost put me off the track forever, I turned left and left again to find myself exactly where I had been five months before: standing in the shadows at the entrance to the Campo dei Gatti.

The furry animals were gathered by the hundreds across the uneven pavement. The door of the Renaissance chapel across the way was still bolted shut, the crumbling wellhead capped for good with its rusty iron cover. And there, in the middle of all that fur, a woman in a black domino setting down newspaper bundles full of restaurant slops. I suppressed an urge to go to her, to take her face in my hands and make my declaration. No, I could find Caterina here now any night. I wanted to find her where she lived, I wanted to find her in her father's house!

I watched silently for some time, as the cats pressed around Caterina's legs, coming to feed. When all the slops were laid out, she sat on the wellhead and instantly her lap was full of cats. She ran her hands across their fur; they pressed against her back, her thighs, two of them clambered to her shoulders. Then she began to sing, a low melancholy song that seemed in tune with their throaty rumblings. She sat in their midst like that for a good hour, white faced, imperturbable, sometimes singing, sometimes not, taken in a sort of cat-inspired trance until the first streaks of dawn showed in the sky to the west. Then she stood abruptly, brushing the cats off of her lap like so many balls of fur, and headed quickly out the opposite end of the campo.

She would be easier to follow than the tabby earlier; in any case, I could easily guess where she was going now: to the Fondamenta Nuove to catch the first vaporetto into the lagoon. If there were enough passengers, I might be able to slip aboard, unnoticed, and follow her all the way home. If not, just knowing which line she took would give me a good idea of her destination—and that was the first step.

I trailed along behind at a safe distance, careful not to scrape my shoes against the pavement. Caterina seemed to have no idea she was being followed. She didn't cast a single backward glance over her shoulder. I felt a little cheap, spying on her like that, and for a moment lost the courage of my overpowering need to know more about her: What if she was a married woman, despite all her protestations to the contrary? A married woman with a jealous husband. What if she were a nun, a lesbian, the mother of ten children? I didn't care. One way or the other, I had to know.

We crossed back over the Mendicanti, headed west for a while along a series of very narrow alleys and came out behind the church of the Gesuiti. I paused in the lee of this baroque structure as she took a sharp right and went out onto the Fondamenta Nuove. I waited here for a minute or two; the Fondamenta Nuove is well lighted and exposed along its whole length. If Caterina just happened to turn around, she would be able to see me coming from a long way off. I would have to wait until she got far enough ahead. At last, I found the right moment, took a deep breath and followed.

Gray light brightened the sky in the east over the city, but the horizon to the west was veiled in night. Blacker storm clouds roiled against the blackness above the walls of the cemetery island riding the swells like a ship at anchor. The lagoon looked rough this morning; three-foot waves swept against the pilings. A few forlorn vessels out of commission for the season stood moored to heavy iron rings fixed into the tarry, waterlogged wood. Only one vaporetto landing showed any activity, the rest were deserted. A crowd of about thirty people waited in the gloom on a platform halfway down. Caterina, walking fast, had just joined their number.

I crept along cautiously, hugging the shadows along the wall, and found refuge in the same doorway in which I had waited for her on the Feast of All Souls. From this distance, I could make out a few faces in the crowd. I saw Caterina's friends Tisiano Naso, the women Bianca and Angelica, and others I now recognized as Barnabotti. It struck me as curious that they should all be taking the same vaporetto at the same time—and a couple of strange scenarios went through my mind: Maybe they lived together in a sort of commune on an outlying island; maybe they were part of a religious cult. After all, for a woman who fucked like a demon, Caterina was very religious. The presence of Caterina's friends now made my situation untenable. Even if I somehow managed to avoid her on the small boat, one of them would recognize me. I would not be able to follow her the rest of the way.

The sky brightened a little more; soon it would be dawn. About ten minutes passed, then the diesel chug of an engine sounded across the lagoon, and a vaporetto rounded the Murano side of San Michele. Everyone waiting on the landing stood absolutely still, backs to the city, staring out into the dark. The beat of the engine coming on and the wind and the waves crashing into the pilings only seemed to increase the empty silence of the morning. I longed for the sound of a human voice, a cough, anything.

Soon, the vaporetto was alongside the landing. The ACTV conductor, dressed in black, jumped down, fixed the mooring line and pulled back the gates, and the Barnabotti began to shuffle aboard. Their white faces looked cold, drained of life; their arms hung listlessly at their sides. It was late or early, depending on your point of view; they were all no doubt drained from the night's excesses. In another minute, everyone was aboard and the gate was up and the vessel lurched out into the swells toward the darkness in the west.

A fine rain began to fall. I waited until the last possible moment, then jumped out of my doorway and ran along the fondamenta until I caught a glimpse of the route card bolted to the side of the main cabin. It was the number 13, an express with no stops, terminating in the lagoon at Sant'Ariano, a place I'd never heard of before. I stood on the edge of the landing and watched the vaporetto disappear around the far side of San Michele, a strange unsettled feeling in the pit of my stomach. The diesel sound sputtered on a little while after that, then it too faded on the wind.

35

RINIO'S VOICE WAS THICK with sleep on the other end of the line. He didn't understand what I was asking. I could hear his wife's annoyed mutter in the background, the baby's gasping cries.

"Giacomo, what time is it?"

I cleared my throat, embarrassed. "I think it's about six-fifteen."

He was confused for a moment. "You mean a.m.? In the morning?"

"Yes, of course, in the morning."

"My God, you call me so early! It is Saturday!"

"I'm sorry about that," I said. "But this is important. I need your help."

"Is it for the bank then, for business?"

"No, Rinio. It's for love."

I could hear him wake up suddenly. "Giacomo, you are a crazy man! Go back to sleep, call me later. She can wait."

"Have you heard of Sant'Ariano?"

He hesitated. The baby's cries grew louder in the background. "You are a very funny person, Giacomo," he said. "Are all Americans so funny?"

"I've looked at a map of the lagoon," I said. "But I can't find it. Do you know where this place is? Sant'Ariano?"

He hesitated again. "Yes," he said.

"I waited two hours for another vaporetto, none came. Will you take me there?"

"You mean in my boat?"

"That's right. The Arkansas Traveller."

"It is much too cold for that kind of sightseeing. In my boat, there is no heat, no cabin. You wait till spring, then we will go."

"I can't wait another minute," I lied. "It's Caterina. I'm supposed to meet her there, at Sant'Ariano. She's running away from her father's house."

Rinio was silent for a moment. Early morning static came over the line, the slow garble of a dozen voices. At last, I heard him sigh.

The day was clear and cold. The rains of the early morning had blown out to sea. A weak winter sun stood at eleven o'clock. The Dolomites showed as vague blue outlines, like mountains in a dream. The Arkansas Traveller cut through the glassy water of the lagoon with a steady sputter. We passed San Michele and Murano and other islands, ramshackle and unnamed, marked by the remains of ancient buildings. A light wind was blowing from the northeast, just cold enough to freeze my hands out of my pockets. My good leather gloves were buried in a trunk in the closet of my bedroom back in the States.

After an hour, we came around the leeward side of Torcello, into the northern neck of the lagoon. Rinio slowed the Traveller to half throttle. The channels through the shallow water here were narrow and poorly marked, clotted with cattails and reeds. The horizon stretched flat and uninteresting all the way to Altino, on the mainland.

"Still, you are very strange, Giacomo!" Rinio said, his breath steaming a cloud in the frigid air. "Sant'Ariano, on a day like this! Is she crazy too, this Vendramin?"

I grinned and filled his mug with hot coffee from the thermos, then added a shot of whiskey from a pint bottle of Vat 69 I had found half submerged in dirty water at the bottom of the built-in aluminum cooler. There was nothing Rinio appreciated more than romantic intrigue, but he was a physical coward. What if there were problems waiting for us at the other end, irate husbands, brothers, cult members? Best not to tell him. In any case, I couldn't really answer his questions. I didn't know myself what I would do when I got to Sant'Ariano—look for Caterina's name on mailboxes, in the local phone book, ask for her father at the local cafe? I just knew I couldn't wait any longer, I had to go there now, today.

"I really do appreciate your help Rinio," I said. "I owe you for this one. Dinner at the Gritti Palace, a new Cadillac, our firstborn child, you name it."

He shrugged. He didn't really seem to mind so much. The trip out into the winter lagoon gave him the chance to wear the expensive purple parka and ski pants he would not wear this year on the slopes. When the coffee ran out, we filled our mugs with the cheap whiskey. I was very nervous. A soft burn that was the beginning of liquid courage began to fill my stomach. Now, the channels were nearly closed by muck and driftwood. We slowed to a crawl and I went forward to push the larger bits out of the way with a grappling hook. The smell of decay seemed to bubble up from the surface of the lagoon.

After another fifteen minutes, we came down a clear channel between two low mudflats that would probably vanish at high tide. Rinio pointed out an uneven wall of dark stone that seemed to rise out of the surface of the lagoon about a quarter of a mile off.

"Where is she?" he said. "I don't see any other boats."

I stepped down into the cockpit and tried to warm my hands on the engine cowling.

"What do you mean?" I said.

He gave me a funny look. "That is Sant'Ariano. We are almost there."

I stood up, bewildered. We were surrounded by nothing, water, mudflats, reeds. Not even the cry of a bird echoed on the wind. "Where are the buildings?" I managed. "The people?"

Rinio almost laughed. "There haven't been any houses here for five hundred years," he said. "Many years ago, I think in the *sedicesimo*, they took all the houses away to make room for that." He pointed again to the distant wall.

I squinted. It looked like nothing, another bit of ruin about to be taken by the lagoon. "This can't be the place." I tried to keep the panic out of my voice. "I mean, she lives there. Her friends live there."

"This is Sant'Ariano, my friend. And I tell you no one lives there."

"No," I said. "That's not possible."

Rinio shrugged. "Since you do not believe me, we will go over and take a look."

Another half hour at slow throttle through the winding channel. Each minute dragged, heavy as lead. At last we motored down an ancient canal almost entirely choked with reeds. The wall ahead proved to be one side of a crumbling enclosure about an acre square, its stone pier lying under five or six feet of greenish water. Before the main gate, a blackened marble angel with a mournful face stood up to her thighs in muck. The stone posterns behind her were leaning away from each other at odd angles, the gate itself long since rusted away.

Rinio maneuvered the Traveller between the posterns and cut the engines. All was silent inside the enclosure. We drifted for a moment and came to rest with a gentle bump against a pile of whitened branches. Then I realized that there were no trees here, and I looked around and saw the branches weren't branches at all but human bones. Mounds and mounds of human bones.

"I think she plays the fool with you," Rinio said, and his voice echoed in the stillness. "As you can see, there's no one here! At least no one alive!" He waved his arms to indicate the desolation all around.

My lips were blue with cold. I could hardly speak. "What is this terrible place?" I said and the question came out a whisper.

"This is Sant'Ariano," Rinio said. "It is an *ossario*, it is the place where they put the bones of the dead people. You see, Venice is very small, and there isn't enough room to bury people in the city, so they bury them on San Michele. San Michele gets so full of bones there is no place to put the new ones. So, unless your family pays more money, or you are famous, they empty all the tombs and the graves and take all the old bones away and they put them here. This whole reef is made of bones. There are many many buried here, too many for anyone to count. There are—"

"This is the only Sant'Ariano?" I interrupted him. "There are no others?"

He shook his head. "There are no others."

"But the vaporetto," I said. "I saw her get on the vaporetto. It was number 13, Sant'Ariano. I saw the route card."

Rino heard the desperation in my voice. "There is no vaporetto that comes here," he said quietly. "As you can see. No one even knows how to find this place anymore. But I know. My grandfather's family, they used to come here in the night and steal the bones to make sugar. Don't ask me how, but they would boil them, grind them, I don't know. The sugar they sold very cheaply, by the kilo in the Rialto market. It was terrible, yes, very bad, but my grandfather was a poor man, a peasant, and he said if the dead can feed the living, why not?"

I leaned over the side and peered into the murky water. Just inches below the surface lay the bones of doges and courtesans, fishwives, children, artists, mothers, daughters, priests, plumbers, gondoliers, merchants, beggars, lovers, fools and all the rest. The Venetian dead of the centuries, greening, eaten by algae, returning to the mire from which they came. *Her father's house has many mansions*, I whispered, and a shudder of horror passed through me as I thought of Caterina's bone-white skin, how it had been free of the slightest blemish and cool to the touch, and I felt very weak suddenly and sick to my stomach and sat down on the red cushions of the boat and put my head in my hands.

"Giacomo, are you ill?" Rinio's voice came to me as a vague echo. Suddenly, I was tired of old stones and an-

cient churches, of the sad whispers of history, of everything that was not new and shiny, of coins that had not
been minted yesterday, of everything that was not plastic
and full of electronic circuitry, of Venice and all her van-
ished splendors and sinking palazzos, and all her rank
lagoons and reedy islands washed slowly into nothing by
the tides. Venice was like a rotting carcass, eaten by
worms, like the body of a woman dead by poison and by
her own hand, just turning blue and beginning to stink. I
gasped for air, I couldn't breathe. Then I felt Rinio's firm
grip on my shoulder.

"We must go back," he said. "There is nothing for you
here."

When I looked up at him, I found my face was wet
with tears.

He clucked sympathetically. "Ah you are very sentimental," he said. "I understand. She has made the fool of
you, this Vendramin, sent you on the chase for a wild
goose. Venetian women are like that, Giacomo, did I not
warn you of this? But think, there are many other women
where she came from. The trick is to make love to them,
but not to fall in love with them."

He went over to the controls, started the engine and
put the Arkansas Traveller into reverse. We inched our
way backward out through the water gate and past the
stone angel with the mournful face, whom I now recognized as the angel of death, and spun around in the
deeper water. Soon the narrow channels gave way to
the open expanse of the lagoon. The wind had died and
the afternoon was warmer, but still cold and very clear. A
formation of mallard ducks crossed above us in a great
wedge, heading south. I wasn't much in the mood for
conversation, so Rinio switched on the radio to a bouncy
Italian pop song, sung by a young woman who sounded

no older than fourteen, and hummed along with the melody.

We swept out into the wide channel at full throttle past Torcello and Burano, and Venice rose like a city in a dream on the horizon all pink and yellow and sepia above the dark green water, its spires and domes flashing in the winter sun. I decided all at once that I didn't know the unexplainable things I knew, and that I would forget about Caterina and about what had happened here. If life teaches us anything, it teaches us how to forget.

EPILOGUE

I AM SITTING EATING my lunch on a granite bench in a piney grove in the Thuya Gardens just above Northeast Harbor, Maine. Lobster boats and white yachts are anchored side by side in the neat little harbor below, the sound of the traffic along 93 reaches me as the vague hum of happy insects. A distant buoy tinkles in a wind from the sea. My lunch consists of a baloney and mayonnaise sandwich, an apple, a bag of barbecued potato chips, and two macaroons. I unwrap the sandwich, careful as a six-year-old on his first day at school, take a bite, then open the bag of chips and munch on a few of these. I am oddly content with my preadolescent lunch, this beautiful day. It has been quite cold here until recently, colder than it ever was in Venice, but today the weatherman says it will reach sixty degrees, and the air is so clear and fresh and good for you I can almost see it sparkling like diamonds as I breathe it into my lungs. I have come down from the lodge to this bench on the overlook to eat my sandwich in the sunlight. Soon, I will climb the slope again and resume my studies. My life is like this right now. I eat lunch alone and spend the days reading about beer.

The Thuya Garden Lodge is home to an extensive library of books on various agrarian topics, among them gardening, animal husbandry, wine making, and the brewing of beer. There are ninety-three titles in the card catalogue regarding the brewing of beer and I intend to read most of them before the summer is done. This is why I have come to Maine, to start up a microbrewery with an old friend from St. John's who lives in Bar Harbor. I have sunk all my worldly assets into the venture. Maine is a good state for microbrews, the laws are lenient, the water is pure, the labor is cheap. There are currently twenty-three different successful small breweries spread across the state, and they include a few nationally distributed brands—Geary's, Salty Dog, Lightship, and Penobscot: respectively, an ale, a lager, a porter, and a stout. My partner and I are not sure what kind of beer to brew yet, though he is leaning toward a strong, Belgian-type ale produced by good old-fashioned bottom fermentation.

At the end of the summer, when I have read all the books there are to read, we will have a better idea. As I sit here, munching on my baloney sandwich, he is in Boston seeing to the purchase of the necessary equipment—giant copper kettles, skimmers, fermenting backs, attemperators, storage kegs, refrigeration pumps, pans for roasting hops, etc., that will allow us to begin production in the fall. I am very serious about beer now, as serious as I have been about anything. In any case, with six hundred and seventy-five dollars remaining in the bank, I have no choice.

Several months have passed since I left Venice. It is June now. In April, Prodi's Olive Tree coalition won 284 seats in the 630-seat chamber of deputies and 167 seats in the 315-seat senate, thus giving them a narrow victory over Berlusconi's Freedom Alliance and initiating a new era in Italian politics. Prodi's first words to jubilant supporters gathered outside Olive Tree headquarters in central Rome were simple: "Be calm." It is advice I have taken to heart. I predicted Olive Tree's sweeping victory in my final report to Capitol Guaranty, filed from Venice in February. But the bank, in the person of Ted Bulley, would not listen.

I learned the fate of my ten-year career as an FX trader over the course of a single curt phone call. Bulley went through all the usual reasons for letting me go: poor trading performance, irrelevant exchange reports—

"Did you read the most current one?" I interrupted.

"No, I don't need to read it," he said, then he dropped the professional tone and I realized he hated me as much as it is possible to hate a man who is not a friend or an enemy. "I'll never know what you said to Warren after I left that time in Milan, but whatever it was, he came back to the hotel a broken man. He looked sick, old, gray. All of a sudden, just like that. My guess is it was caused by something you said. I usually feel sorry for the fuckups the bank terminates, but not for you, you bastard. Firing you gives me a hard-on."

I could hear the venom in his voice, the ambition and greed wrapped in tight coils inside him. And I closed my eyes and could see his body at its patient work of destroying itself, his guts slowly curdling like sour milk.

"If you don't watch yourself, Ted," I said, trying to sound as reasonable as possible, "you'll go the same way Warren went—in pain, wondering why. You're already halfway there. You should listen to me, I know these things." I hung up before he had a chance to give vent to his smug, self-righteous anger.

Ted Bulley's demise came sooner than I thought; it was not the death of his body, but the death of his career, which to him would be worse. On his recommendation, the board instructed traders at Capitol Guaranty to unload twenty billion dollars' worth of lire two days before the Italian elections. Bulley actually assumed correctly that the left would win, but he also assumed the world economic community would be depressed about it. He was wrong. Italian enthusiasm for their new government was infectious; and this infectiousness spread like a disease to the world financial markets. After all, who does not love Italy—the food, the wine, the women, the climate, the antiquities—and wish her well? Following the elections, the lira shot up quickly to 1980 levels against the dollar and the bank went short in a drastic way; in layman's terms, the bank was caught with its pants down and lost a shitload of money.

I followed the fiasco in the financial pages of *The Boston Globe*; at this very moment, heads are rolling at high levels. Bulley, I have no doubt, was the first to go. There is even some talk that Comparini International will be bought out by the mighty Tobiko Bank of Japan. But I am done with all that. I have sold my town house in Arlington Mews, my Saab Turbo convertible, all but one of my eight-hundred-dollar suits. I rent the downstairs of a small turn-of-the-century house in Bar Harbor, my partner rents the upstairs, and the owner, an old woman known only as Mrs. Lawrence, lives in the back. Now, my life is beer.

Beer is a much more complicated matter than one would think. Beer, I have become fond of saying, is a science. And, of course, like most sciences, it is also an art.

"There can be little doubt that every nation evolves a type of beer most suited to the climate and the temperament of its people," say J. L. Baker and P. Schidrowitz in their classic work, *Mild Ales*. Baker and Schidrowitz knew wisdom when they drank it. Beer also, is one of the oldest of man's endeavors. In *Beer—A Short History*, Arthur Doemens traces beer back to the very beginnings of civilization. According to Doemens, beer may in fact be responsible for civilization itself:

"The communal effort necessary for the production of beer gave early man a compelling reason to put aside the continual warfare and mutual distrust that ruled his days; to step more than one foot beyond his weapons, set his shoulder to the grinding wheels, his hands to the fermentation pots."

Doemens is a little hyperbolic in his praise of the beverage, but archeologists have recently discovered the remains of an eight-thousand-year-old brewery in Egypt. I suppose, in a way, beer can be blamed for all the unfortunate complexities that followed, including safety pins, underwear, and the Internet—and perhaps even the imminent collapse of Capitol Guaranty.

The crisp spring nights up here are good for sleeping. My insomnia is receding like an evil tide. Most nights I manage to get five or six uninterrupted hours. But my sleep is still haunted by disturbing dreams, which often seem to combine an odd mixture of erotic and funerary imagery. I dream of Caterina's white body beneath my own; we are making love in dusty tombs full of bones, on fallen gravestones whose inscriptions have been effaced by time, in battered silk-lined coffins, in the backs of hearses on the way to crumbling ossuaries rising out of the middle of Frenchman Bay. I am also frequently visited in sleep by Elizabeth, favorite cat of the spirit world.

Here in Maine, she is not the wet, rotting horror of earlier nightmares, but a normal, fluffy kitty escaped from the jaws of death and my perforated biscuit tin still furry and warm, and somehow endowed with the gift of speech. When she speaks, she sounds just like my mother, and her message is always the same:

"Nothing will ever be as it was with you," she says. "You have drunk wine with the dead, you have eaten a meal at their very table, you have lain with them in cold embrace, you have—"

At this point, I put my hands over my ears and begin to scream. At least once the screams turned real and I woke old Mrs. Lawrence in the back room. She pounded on the wall with her rubber-tipped cane and I got up, pajama top stuck to my back with sweat, my neck cold, to read back issues of *Beer Digest* at the dining room table until dawn.

Mrs. Lawrence, I am sure, does not like me much. She only tolerates my presence in her house because of my partner, whom she loves like the son she never had. She thinks I am crazy or a drunk or worse—that I have some great sin on my conscience that prevents me from looking her in the eye. It is true, I will not look her in the eye, but this is only because I do not care to know exactly when she will drop dead. The gift or curse, acquired, I suspect, like a metaphysical venereal disease, from sleeping with Caterina, will not go away. So, I avoid old people and sickrooms; I would not visit my partner in the hospital when he fell off a ladder at our newly rented warehouse and broke his hip.

That last cold day out on the lagoon, I vowed to forget about Caterina, but of course this has proven impossible. I am more determined than ever to get to the bottom of the mystery surrounding her. When I am not reading about beer, I dip into my growing private library of Venetiana purchased since March at used-book stores in Washington, New York, and Boston. I now own over forty-five volumes dealing with Venetian history, art, and architecture, including rare copies of Sarpi's *Considera-*

zioni sulle censure and *Maxims*, Pascolato's *Life of Sarpi*, the *Life and Letters of Sir Henry Wooton, Ambassador to the Serenissima*, Thomas Nashe's *The Unfortunate Traveller*, Foscarini's *History of Venetian Literature*, Addison's *Remarks on Several Parts of Italy*, Goldoni's *Mémoires*, Dickens's *Pictures from Italy*, Ruskin's *Stones of Venice*, Beckford's *Dreams, Waking Thoughts and Incidents*—just to name a few.

And finally, there is the letter—a single piece of heavy stationery folded twice and sealed with a familiar crest in red wax—which was forwarded to me from the Palazzo Bragadino three months ago. The stationery still bears the last vestiges of her scent, the faint, erotic perfume of funerary lilies; the words are written in pale ink, which is already fading, in a curious, ornate script that one day soon I intend to submit to a handwriting expert:

Darling Jack—

I am sorry my Darling if you have been wondering about me, where I am, but you must never see me again. I could not resist these last words, only so you would not hate me so much. My Father has told me to go away, and go I must. I do not have the power to disobey Him. I am sad not to see you again and I am sad that no one will feed the cats when I am gone. You have asked me once if I am married. The answer is both yes and no. I cannot explain any better, I have already said too much. But you must know that I think of you always. You have made my heart live again and for this I am grateful. You have given me the only pleasure I have known in many long years. Forget me and leave me to my darkness. I am tired now.

Ti amo, Caterina

190

On one hand, as she suggests, Caterina will always remain a mystery of the profoundest kind. On the other hand, if I abandon a few of the conceptions of reality maintained throughout my whole rational life—that God does not exist, that the universe is a meaningless, random place, that when people are dead, they stay dead—then certain complex explanations follow, all beginning and ending with Paulo Sarpi.

Caterina, Tisiano Naso, and the rest of the Barnabotti called Sarpi a saint. Perhaps he was a saint, though he is not recognized as such officially by the Catholic Church. No miracles are attributed to his name, except that the poisoned dagger driven through his cheek by papal assassins was later tested on a dog, who died instantly. Instead, Sarpi spent his life fighting the inequities of this world. He fought the Inquisition, the dogmatic tyrannies of Rome, the selling of benefices and various other corruptions in an era of bad religious practices and worse popes. He lived a selfless life, devoted to an unlikely trinity—to God, to the pursuit of knowledge, and to Venice.

It was said that Sarpi loved his native city more than any other man has loved a place. When forced to leave the islands of the Rialto for a few days, he would weep, become physically ill. Sarpi loved Venice so much, according to Micanzio's *Life*, he might easily have been able to convince God it was a more beautiful place than Paradise. In a way, this was perhaps exactly what had happened. On his deathbed in 1623, Sarpi was heard to utter a prayer for his beloved city. *"Esto perpetua . . ."* he prayed, "may she live forever." They were his last words. God has a habit of honoring the dying wishes of His saints. Look at Venice now; Sarpi's singular miracle is more than obvious. The pilings beneath most of Venice's buildings have rotted away completely; recent sonograms published in *National Geographic* show the hidden damage. High tides eat away at her alleys and campos several times a year; there are the combined effects of chemical pollution, acid rain, and the wake of motorboats pounding her disintegrating foundations, but the city continues to loom over the waters of the lagoon in defiance of gravity and physics and time. As if held up by golden chains bound to heaven.

Still, as Rinio once said, what is a city, if not the people in it? What is Venice without the peculiar, inventive race of men and women that built her up from the mud and reeds of the lagoon? Why, indeed, would God want to preserve a city full of tourists? It is true, only a handful of real Venetians remain, that is, those citizens who can trace their ancestry back for more than five generations of Venice's long history. And only these few stand between Venice and its inevitable monstrous half-life as the next Euro Disney. And yet miraculously, Venice is still Venice. How has it managed to stay so much itself, despite the depredations of Coca-Cola and backpackers and other indignities of the twentieth century?

If I follow my reasoning to the end, the answer to this question is sinister, macabre and ridiculous at the same time: since it was once the duty of the Barnabotti to serve Venice in life, why not in death? As long as the Barnabotti remain, Venice remains. They are the undead spirit of the city, its one thousand five hundred years personified, its triumphs and days of glory and long, splendid decline, all of which belong inexorably to the past. Life after death in Venice seems excruciating to me, though I suppose there are worse places to spend the allotted span in purgatory.

But for Caterina and the rest of them, Venice must resemble a big, creaky amusement park with all the rides closed for repair forever. They wander its shadowy alleys and ruined palazzos praying for release, desperate for that final sleep; the memories of life like a vague and ancient dream. They are flesh but not flesh, they are allowed a few pleasures—a drink, a little gambling, a puff or two of hash, a love affair—to alleviate the stultifying boredom of the passing centuries.

Unlike Sarpi, I am no theologian. My grasp of metaphysical matters is shaky at best. Dead flesh come alive again, this is the stuff of horror movies and the Bible. I thought it best to get a professional opinion.

Around the corner from my place in Bar Harbor is St. Michael's, a small red-brick Catholic church that serves the few parishioners who remain on Mt. Desert Island after the summer people have gone. The priest, Father Ian McBride, is a recent transplant from Ireland. Today, after I leave the Thuya library, I put on my only remaining sport jacket, a jaunty plaid number, and stroll around to see him. The afternoon is mild and bright. Gulls shriek in the sky overhead. I can hear the thick foghorn of the *Bluenose*, the ferry from Nova Scotia, sounding from the strand at the foot of Main Street.

I find Father McBride dressed in a T-shirt and jeans, on his knees in the garden of the rectory, a little yellow cottage separated from the street by a high hedge of English boxwood. He is planting a newly dug bed of annuals—impatiens, petunias, marigolds—and when I come around the hedge, he stands, brushes the dirt from his knees, takes off his gardening gloves and offers his hand. He is a thin man in his early forties, with a soft Dublin lilt to his speech, sandy hair, and washed-out blue eyes. I identify myself as a Catholic and we chat about flowers, worms, the weather, then I get around to the point of my visit.

"Father, I was wondering . . ." I hesitate, a little embarrassed. "I was wondering if you could answer a few theological questions?"

He frowns. "Theological? What do you mean?"

I squint up at the dark knob of Cadillac Mountain and back down at the freshly turned earth at my feet. I don't really know where to begin.

Father McBride puts a hand on my shoulder. "You better come inside," he says.

We go through the screen door into the cottage's spotless, 1950s-era kitchen. I see a heavy, ceramic Sears Kenmore stove, an ancient Frigidaire with the cooler coil on top, and a turquoise Formica-and-chrome dinette set with four turquoise and chrome chairs. Above the stove, on the wall, hangs a 3-D rendition of the *Last Supper* in a beige plastic frame.

"I'll admit that's not really to my taste," he says, indicating the 3-D *Last Supper*, "but I'd feel a little guilty taking it down." He makes coffee in a battered aluminum pot on the stove, fills two cups and sets them down on the Formica table. We sit and drink our coffee in silence for a minute. Finally, he leans back and waits for me to speak.

I tell him about Caterina, and about Venice, about the strange end to our affair and about my newly acquired gift. He listens without comment, without surprise or incredulity on his face, his blue eyes unreadable. I get the feeling he's heard many strange stories in his years as a priest.

"So, do you think, Father"—I don't quite know how to

put this in less dramatic terms—"that the dead can be brought back to life, that crumbling bones can take on flesh and walk again? That dead mouths can speak? And who do you think"—my words catch in my throat; when they come out again, they come out a bare whisper—"and who do you think can perform this dreadful miracle?"

The priest is silent for a while, considering. Then he sits up straight and folds his hands on the table, a reflex I recognize from Catholic school.

"As good Christians, we must believe that the Lord in His ultimate wisdom can do many things that we might find incredible, and that might seem contrary to the laws of nature," he says in a clear voice that is only vaguely preachy. "Think of the walls of Jericho, tumbling down at the single blast of a trumpet, think of how He made the sun stop in its diurnal course for the benefit of Joshua and the Israelites. And think of that other occasion, which we both know so well, when He harrowed hell itself to bring his only son back from death to the world of the living.

"Contemplate these mysteries, if you will, Mr. Squire. But let me hasten to add, that if you are contemplating them in hopes of reaching a rational understanding, then you are committing a very grave error indeed. Your odd experiences in Venice may come under this category— the unknowable. And the best we poor sinners can do in the face of the unknowable is to trust in God and try even harder to live a good and worthy life. From here on out, I advise you to concern yourself with more earthly matters."

Then he pauses, a little red in the face, and draws a deep breath. Like many modern priests, he is uncomfortable talking about God. "Let me ask you something now, are you a member of this parish?"

"I live just around the corner, if that's what you mean," I say.

Father McBride seems a little put out by this. "That's not at all what I mean," he says. "What I mean is we need to see your butt in the pew for Sunday mass, every Sunday. And before you can come to mass, you'll need to come to confession, which, for your information, is held every Wednesday from ten in the morning till two in the afternoon. Because if, as you say, you pursued sexual relations with that Venetian woman outside the sanctity of marriage, it's still adultery plain and simple, even if she was dead when you did it. And adultery is a mortal sin. Do you understand?"

After an embarrassed moment I mumble that I do, then he smiles makes me promise to come in for confession the following Wednesday, and we go back out into the garden, and he walks me down the gravel drive to the sidewalk.

"And what is it that you're doing here among us?" he asks me as an afterthought.

"You mean here in Bar Harbor, in Maine?"

"Yes, I always like to know what they're up to, my *parishioners*," he says, emphasizing the last word.

"I'm here to make beer," I say. "My partner and I are going to start up a microbrew. We've already rented a warehouse in Town Hill. He's in Boston getting estimates on the equipment right now."

His eyes light up at this. "Ah, beer is it? I'm a great fan of a nice pint every now and then—in moderation of course."

"Of course."

"And what sort of beer do you have in mind to make?"

I shrug. "A lager, maybe. Or a Belgian-style ale. Or maybe a stout. We haven't decided yet."

The priest scratches his chin, thinking. "Well, if you're asking me, I fancy a good, hearty stout," he says at last.

And we shake hands and leave it at that.